Flight of Fancy

A Clara Fitzgerald Mystery

Evelyn James

Red Raven Publications 2023
www.sophie-jackson.com

Contents

Chapter One	1
Chapter Two	8
Chapter Three	14
Chapter Four	22
Chapter Five	30
Chapter Six	38
Chapter Seven	47
Chapter Eight	58
Chapter Nine	66
Chapter Ten	72
Chapter Eleven	82
Chapter Twelve	90
Chapter Thirteen	97
Chapter Fourteen	104
Chapter Fifteen	114
Chapter Sixteen	123
Chapter Seventeen	131
Chapter Eighteen	139

Chapter Nineteen	147
Chapter Twenty	156
Chapter Twenty-One	165
Chapter Twenty-Two	173
Chapter Twenty-Three	183
Chapter Twenty-Four	192
Chapter Twenty-Five	199
Chapter Twenty-Six	207
Chapter Twenty-Seven	214
Chapter Twenty-Eight	226
Enjoyed this Book?	234
The Clara Fitzgerald Series	235
Also by Evelyn James	238
About the Author	239
Copyright	240

Chapter One

Over Brighton pier, the biplane swooped as gracefully as a bird, startling several onlookers who gasped appreciatively.

"Poetry in motion," Tommy Fitzgerald murmured as he sat in his wheelchair and watched the aerial performance.

"Had I still got the use of these," he tapped his crippled legs, "I would be up in one of those in a second."

"And giving your poor sister nightmares," Annie, the Fitzgeralds' unconventional maid gave a shudder of horror at the thought of being in a plane.

Clara Fitzgerald, meanwhile, was a few paces away scanning the sky with an old pair of binoculars. It was the first time she had seen a plane flying, though she had read enough about them in the papers and the war had been full of daring aeronautical exploits, but that was so different from seeing the thing up close.

She heard a loud bang beside her and turned sharply.

"Oliver Bankes!"

Oliver Bankes, police photographer and proprietor of the Bankes' Photographic Studios, hauled himself out from under the black cloth draped on the back of his camera and looked apologetic.

"I've never photographed a plane before. It's exceptionally hard," he mumbled under the steady gaze of Clara. "I do think I missed it once again, predicting where the plane will be in the sky is quite a bother and, really, I don't think the camera can take the shot fast enough."

"Why don't you just enjoy watching it then? Instead of making all that racket and light?"

"But that's not the point, is it?" Oliver said mournfully. "It's the artist inside me, just like a painter sees a scene and has to capture it on canvas, so I see that plane and desperately want to capture it on a glass plate."

"You can never capture *that*," Clara motioned to the plane as it did a nippy turn and dashed over the ocean yet again, so low to the waves it seemed close to skimming them. "Not even a moving picture could do it. You have to be here, seeing it with your own eyes, soaking up the excited atmosphere, smelling the foul engine fuel and the reek of the sea."

"I did not know you enjoyed aviation, Miss Fitzgerald."

"You wouldn't get me in a plane, but I *am* curious about this new technology."

"They predict soon we will all be flying everywhere in the things," Oliver took a pause from his camera to watch the plane do an impressive mid-air twist. "Last year there was that non-stop transatlantic flight made by Alcock and Brown."

"Yes, but *His Majesty's Airship R34* made the first crossings of the Atlantic, going from Scotland to New York and then back to England. Quite frankly, if one must travel by air, I would much prefer an airship to these scrawny biplanes. They seem infinitely safer."

"I say, he is going to land!" Oliver grabbed his camera with its wooden tripod and raced with the crowd to the edge of the pier to get a better look.

The little biplane took one last turn then came down in a steep dive aiming for a straight tract of sand which had been freshly raked (under the scrutiny of the plane's pilot) that morning. The plane looked fit to crash to Clara's eyes, but as the ground raced up its small wheels touched down with the gentleness of a caress and within minutes the plane was drifting to a halt in a cloud of yellow dust.

A cheer went up from the pier and a round of applause rippled through the audience as the pilot of the plane emerged from his craft and gave everyone a hearty wave.

"Captain O'Harris," Oliver informed Clara. "I hear he is aiming to make his own transatlantic crossing in half the time of Alcock and Brown!"

"Is that feasible?"

"I don't know, but if I got a picture of him in front of his plane and then he actually made the flight I could sell the shot to all the papers," Oliver was snatching up his camera again and racing for the stairs of the pier.

Several people were doing the same and cries of "Captain O'Harris, Captain O'Harris" echoed across the sand.

"A load of fuss over a man who hasn't the sense to have a real job," Annie tutted loudly, wheeling Tommy to join Clara.

"He is at the forefront of aviation Annie, imagine the possibilities!" Tommy objected.

"All I saw was a young man showing off," Annie said firmly. "Quite frankly, I would rather have stayed at home and made the fruit cake I've been saving all those currants for."

Clara smiled at the pair of them.

"Care to meet the famous O'Harris?" She said to her brother.

Tommy glanced over the edge of the pier and looked uncertain.

"Not nervous, are you?" Clara asked, sensing his reluctance.

"Just feeling like a bit of a lame duck next to a graceful swan, is all," Her brother responded.

"Nonsense!" Clara shook her head. "Don't be ashamed of yourself Tommy. You fought for this country so the likes of Mr O'Harris could fly his plane over a free England. You sacrificed your legs for him, nothing to be ashamed of in that."

Tommy looked grim.

"Doesn't feel like that."

"Well, I fancy meeting him," Clara declared. "Not every day I get to talk to a pilot."

She sauntered along the pier and headed among the crowd. Captain O'Harris had his audience in the palm of his hand as he regaled them with stories of adventures in his plane.

"...there we were, in the desert, supposedly trying out the old girl in speed tests and the blooming engine clogged with sand and we were stuck with no water and miles from our base camp! Jolly lucky, our guides came to find us."

"Captain O'Harris, a photo perhaps?" Oliver called out.

O'Harris gave a modest look of abashment to the crowd and then walked over to his plane and took up a rather too well-rehearsed pose to convince Clara that he really was not used to such attention. She edged her way through the crowd, observing O'Harris in his cream flying overalls and leather flying cap. He had a beaming grin stuck to his face and fondly patted The *White Buzzard*, his personal biplane. Oliver's camera gave a flash, and the moment was captured as he had hoped.

"Captain O'Harris, is it true you intend to fly to New York?" Someone called out.

"Why yes," O'Harris beamed, "I intend to break the Alcock and Brown record with just myself and a co-pilot flying."

"Isn't that extremely dangerous?" Clara piped up.

O'Harris turned his radiant gaze on her and for a second she was disconcerted by his smile.

"Now why would you say that?" He asked.

"Even supposing you can manage to get enough fuel aboard, and your plane looks a good deal smaller than that used by Alcock and Brown, you have to take into account technical faults, difficulties with the weather and human fatigue. Not to mention I believe you intend to fly from Brighton? Alcock and Brown chose to go from Newfoundland in the US to Ireland, a shorter distance."

O'Harris had a twinkle in his eye.

"You are very well-informed," he grinned. "An aviation enthusiast, perhaps?"

"That's Clara Fitzgerald!" A woman announced nearby. "She is Brighton's first female private detective, maybe even Britain's first!"

Clara was humbled to have been recognised.

"Have you been doing some detecting on me, Miss Fitzgerald?" O'Harris asked.

"Not specifically," Clara muttered, fearing she was blushing. "But I have become quite curious about aviation since the war."

"There ain't much Clara Fitzgerald don't know about," the woman, apparently Clara's unofficial publicist, said dramatically. "She has the mind of a man, but the instincts of a woman. She solved the murder of Mrs Greengage back in January, quite when the police were at a dead end."

Clara noted that Captain O'Harris seemed suddenly even more intrigued by her. In contrast, she wanted to slip away into the crowd.

"To answer your question Miss Fitzgerald, yes it will be dangerous, but worth the risk if we can set a new record and push the boundaries of aviation. Why, I do not think it will be many more years before planes become as common a form of transport as the automobile."

This statement raised a whole host of new questions from the crowd and Clara was relieved to be able to slip away and return to Tommy on the pier.

"Well, what is he like?" Her brother asked as she appeared.

"Over-confident," Clara shrugged. "Alcock and Brown were lucky, a month before their attempt the American navy had planned a similar flight with stops built into the journey. Of the three seaplanes they sent only one made it and they were supported by a trail of Station Ships, which acted as navigational markers for the pilots."

"So, you think he can't do it?"

"I don't say that, but I think it is highly dangerous for very little reward. We know it's possible, so why do it again?"

"I would give it a go, if I could," admitted Tommy.

"Well, I have to say I am very glad you can't Tommy Fitzgerald," Annie said, clutching at his shoulder. "Those planes give me quite the horrors, my stomach flips right over when he does them turns."

"It's safer than you think Annie," Clara assured her.

"Would you go up in one of those contraptions Miss Fitzgerald?"

Clara felt a shiver ripple down her spine.

"Certainly not."

"Well, you may have to revise that statement, old thing, because the good captain is heading our way," remarked Tommy. "Would you still refuse to go if he asked you?"

"Absolutely," Clara said staunchly, turning around to see Captain O'Harris heading along the pier towards them.

"Couldn't let you get away quite like that Miss Fitzgerald," O'Harris grinned as he drew close. "I'm having a luncheon for select residents of Brighton tomorrow and wondered if you would care to join me? Of course, the invitation extends to your husband as well."

O'Harris' gaze had slipped to Tommy.

"This is my older brother, Thomas," Clara explained hastily. "And I believe we would both be most delighted to join you tomorrow."

"Excellent!" O'Harris' grin managed to get broader. "See you about noon then?"

He sauntered off, stopping to speak to various adoring fans as he went.

"Quite the character," Tommy remarked as he vanished from sight.

"Yes," said Annie. "And didn't he look pleased when he found out you were Miss Fitzgerald's brother and not her husband!"

Clara gave them both a disapproving look.

Chapter Two

"And this is the dining room," O'Harris escorted his guests into an expansive room with tall glass windows lining the length of the back wall and giving fine views over the immaculate gardens and grounds. You did not get very far in aeronautics without a substantial private income.

"This is certainly impressive," Tommy nodded, casting an eye over the other guests assembled at the impromptu luncheon, he knew a few of them including the mayor of Brighton, but most were complete strangers to him.

"Don't be fooled by appearances, old boy," O'Harris chortled. "The roof forever leaks no matter how often it's fixed and the draughts about this place in winter would freeze the fur off a polar bear! Can't get the whole house warm for love nor money, that's why I spend the winters in Spain tweaking the *Buzzard's* engines."

"Still, this is a fine family home," The mayor piped up approvingly, he was fund-raising again for the Pavilion and could see an opportunity when it stood before him. "I imagine you, ah, inherited quite a fortune from the late Mrs O'Harris?"

"Poor dead Aunt Flo," O'Harris sighed. "Quite miss the old battle-axe. I was her only nephew you see."

"Yes," said the mayor, feeling his subject was hooked. "And she was very fond of philanthropic endeavours…"

"I say, is this Doulton?" Distracted by another guest eyeing up his crockery, O'Harris moved away much to the mayor's disappointment.

Clara wheeled her brother to the window and stared out into the gardens. Hazy sunshine was making up for a morning of rain and the grounds looked inviting in the yellow light.

"Lucky Captain O'Harris," Tommy mused.

"In my experience luck can be fickle," Clara replied.

Dinner was served a little after one and, despite O'Harris' claims that it would be a light luncheon, the guests were presented with a series of courses fit for an evening soiree. Soup was followed by fish, and then a game pie, followed by cheeses and ending with an array of exquisite looking desserts. Each course was preceded by a small bowl of chilled sorbet, enough to cleanse the palate for the next dish.

Clara had not seen food on such a scale since before the war and she noted that several other people were the same. She took care with each course not to consume too much, but not all were so sensible and by dessert several guests looked stuffed to their gills. The temptation to glut themselves on the fish, and game pie had just been too great.

O'Harris held sway over his dinner table like he did over everything else.

"Imagine a plane big enough to hold twenty people like an airship, or maybe more, maybe 100!" He told a lady beside him.

"Oh, dear Captain, I think you do take these concepts too far," the lady's male companion responded.

"Nonsense, it's entirely feasible."

"But what about the size? You surely can't expect one hundred people to sit in little cockpits like you and your co-pilot do."

"It would be like a coach with wings, nothing remarkable in that. It's all about aerodynamics. Get the thrust and the proportions right and, boom, it's all yours! Isn't that right Miss Fitzgerald?"

Clara glanced up at her name being called. She was seated close enough to the captain to have heard most of the conversation, but it would have been impolite to admit she had been listening.

"What is right, Mr O'Harris?"

"That in the future there will be planes that can carry a 100 people, maybe even more!"

"Absurd! Absurd!" Chuckled the unconvinced male guest, but Clara let the question sink in for a moment.

"I suppose it might be a possibility. Given resources and time, but a plane that large would need a landing strip of some description. Fields and beaches could no longer be relied upon," she answered.

"Quite, it will need an air terminal, like the military had during the war. A harbour for planes if you will."

"This is all fantasy, honestly," the male guest shook his head in amusement. "I am impressed with your imagination, but truly there is nothing rational in what you say."

O'Harris looked mildly perturbed, but he laughed along with his guest anyway.

Later, tea was served to the guests who milled around the dining room, taking in the views, and overcoming lunch. Clara stood by a tall window gazing at the first signs of spring flowers emerging in the garden. For a moment she didn't realise O'Harris had joined her until he spoke.

"Unimaginative lot, aren't they?"

She glanced at him.

"Don't get me wrong," O'Harris continued, "all good souls, but they can't lift their heads above the parapet for a second. They don't see the potential. Quite frankly Miss Fitzgerald I think I would have gone out of my mind had I not had the fortune to invite yourself and Mr Fitzgerald."

Clara smiled.

"Are you suggesting I lift my head above the parapet?"

"Lift? You, my dear, you are truly flying!"

Clara felt herself blushing again, it was uncharacteristic.

"I think you overestimate me."

"Nonsense! A female detective in Brighton! You are unique, dare I say, innovative, special even."

"You flatter me."

"Isn't it the truth though?"

Clara looked away out the window, not certain of how to respond.

"I have a hunch it won't be many years before you see female pilots making transatlantic crossings," O'Harris continued, diverting the subject.

"That would be something to see," mused Clara.

"Of course, it's rather an old boy's network at the moment. Very much a case of who you know and how much money you've got. Too many folks don't think there is a future in planes and the ones that do, well, let's just say they have a tendency to be old-fashioned in their thinking except when it comes to aeronautics."

"They would make it difficult for women?"

"I should say! Some of the best trainers wouldn't want to teach a lady, but it will happen, mark my words. I just hope it doesn't take another war for them to realise the value of female pilots. It took the Great War to get them to see the worth in planes!"

Clara nodded thoughtfully.

"I could take you up, if you would like?"

Clara almost spilled her tea at the suggestion.

"In a plane?"

"In old *Buzzard*."

"I fear not Mr O'Harris," Clara said, trying to pretend she had not gone quite pale. "I am inclined to keep my feet firmly on the ground."

"She really is quite safe."

"Even so."

O'Harris laughed.

"I supposed she does seem a bit of a schoolboy's project in comparison to the automobile and the train. But she has to be light, you see."

"I quite understand but forgive me if I would rather entrust my safety to the pavement than to a vehicle constructed of paper and wood."

"Don't call her a vehicle," O'Harris purred, putting on a pretence of hurt. "She is a thing of grace and beauty; she is an aeroplane – as far removed from those clunky automobiles people swear are the latest thing as a bird is from a horse! She is freedom, she is…"

O'Harris faltered for words briefly.

"She is everything I ever dreamed of as a boy. When I was trapped in that dreary boarding school, wishing the days away until I could break free, I could only half imagine the adventures I would eventually live. Flying during the war, weaving in and out of the old Hun, getting the scoop on the battlefields below for the boys in the trenches. We lived every moment waiting for a stray bullet to cast us down into No Man's Land, yet no sooner did I land then I wanted to be up in the air again. I have been addicted to flight ever since."

"It sounds as though you are not the sort of man to live a quiet life," Clara observed.

"No, I suppose not," O'Harris grinned.

Distantly a clock in the hallway chimed the hour.

"I've asked a handful of guests to stay on for a drink in the drawing room and perhaps a hand of bridge by the fire, I would welcome an extra lady to the party," O'Harris' charm was infectious.

"That sounds delightful."

"Then you will be my bridge partner?"

"I don't play."

"But I suspect, dear lady, with your mind you could pick up the game in an instant."

Clara was amused.

"No wonder the old *Buzzard* works so well for you, if you show her half as much charm as you are showing me."

"The *Buzzard* is fond of her master," O'Harris winked. "But like most decent women she can be fickle with her love."

He offered his arm to Clara, who took it, not knowing quite how to respond.

Chapter Three

"Wasn't this the old boy's study?" Remarked Colonel Brandt, casting his eye around the smaller drawing room O'Harris had escorted his chosen guests to. "It took me a moment but, yes, I am sure of it. This was his study. I used to visit him here, oh, a good twenty years ago!"

"You are referring to my Uncle Goddard," O'Harris said, placing a glass of brandy by the colonel's chair.

"That I am. Fine fellow, always good to his visitors. I used to come here when I was working with my father at his surgery. Used to bring Goddard's rheumatics pills personally. He used to regale me with stories of the Boer war, and I was so taken I ended up joining the service quite to father's dismay."

"Oh yes, I remember too," piped up Mrs Rhone who had come accompanying her husband, who was a reverend at Margate. "I was a Brighton girl and I do recall that Mr Goddard O'Harris used to always help out at the summer fete and parades. He was a rather good horseman, I believe, and liked to ride at the head of any marching event."

"Poor Uncle Goddard," sighed Captain O'Harris, settling himself into a chair with a glass of port. "Auntie Flo tore him to pieces most days, can't quite imagine why he married her."

"It was love, Captain," Mrs Rhone added. "I was only a girl, but I do remember the day they were wed, and it was quite spectacular. Florence was so excited and happy she cried on the church steps. Such a shame how it all ended. It must have broken your aunt's poor heart."

"I think auntie was made of sterner stuff than that," winked O'Harris.

"But did they ever work out what happened?" Colonel Brandt asked.

"No, quite the mystery," O'Harris shrugged his shoulders. "All I know is auntie had this room rearranged before he was cold in the ground, metaphorically speaking of course."

"It was the shock," Mrs Rhone said sympathetically.

"If you say so," O'Harris took a glug of port. "But here, look, we have one of the first-rate detectives in Brighton in our midst and we haven't even asked her opinion!"

Clara looked up at the handful of guests who had turned to her rather eagerly.

"I'm afraid you have me at a loss," she said. "I do not know what mystery you are referring to?"

"Surely everyone knows the Goddard O'Harris mystery!" Mrs Rhone was stunned.

"I, unfortunately, do not."

"Quite understandable," the colonel nodded. "Before your time and once the matter was over with, only us old souls who remembered it bothered to talk about it. Florence O'Harris kept tight-lipped on the subject."

A general air of disappointment descended on the audience.

"However, if you would care to give me the facts of the matter, I would certainly be interested," Clara suggested.

"The facts are really quite straightforward Miss Fitzgerald," O'Harris emptied his glass and eased himself further into the chair. "My uncle Goddard died one day in the garden and then he, quite simply, vanished."

There was a pause.

"Vanished?" Queried Clara.

"Into thin air, between the span of time it took for my Aunt Florence to rush indoors and call a servant to fetch a doctor and then to go out in the garden again."

"Perhaps he was not dead?" Clara offered.

"Oh, but he was," interjected the colonel. "I saw him meself. Dead as a dodo. His face twisted in horror and grey as ash. You see, while poor Florence O'Harris ran for the servants, I ran for the police. If ever I saw a man murdered in me life, I saw him that day."

Clara put down her own glass of sherry, her curiosity piqued.

"I think this needs some clarification; a man died, possibly murdered, and then the body evaporated into thin air? Did the police do a search?"

"Of course, once they concluded I wasn't lying. I dare say they thought I had had a little too much of the good brandy. Talking of which?" Colonel Brandt waggled his glass at O'Harris who obediently filled it.

"I see we have your attention Miss Fitzgerald, perhaps you would care for me to explain in greater detail?"

"I am certainly interested," Clara agreed. "It is a rather odd mystery. And no one has ever solved it?"

"Far as I am aware, aside from the police and, I suppose, Auntie Flo, no one has ever bothered to try," O'Harris shrugged. "Still, it makes a rather good fireside story with the evening drawing in."

"Oh, do tell the tale," Mrs Rhone clapped her hands together keenly. "I would love to hear Miss Fitzgerald's perspective on this little mystery that has quite troubled me all these years."

"I do not promise a solution," Clara protested.

"Just give your opinion," Colonel Brandt added. "Can't hurt. O'Harris, tell the story."

Captain O'Harris crossed his legs and poured himself another port.

"I suppose I should do that old story telling lark and say it began like this," he grinned. "Goddard O'Harris married Florence Highgrove in 1868. Typical Victorian wedding as Mrs Rhone will tell you."

"My dear it was beautiful!" Mrs Rhone obediently commented. "I was a mere girl, but Goddard was so dashing and Florence the perfect blushing bride. I remember the carriage all decked in flowers and pulled by pairs of roan geldings."

"So, you see, it all started well enough," O'Harris regained the conversation. "And I imagine it went the way most marriages do. They got on all right, far as I could tell, not that I knew them until the 1890s, of course, by then they seemed quite old to me. My father, Goddard's brother, was a decade younger than him you see, so by the time I was on the scene and old enough to take account of anything they were both in their fifties. I dare say father had caused them some strife in his time, he was rather like me and too fond of adventure to be terribly sensible and he married mother quite on a whim and she was deemed by the O'Harris clan as eminently unsuitable."

"Dear me, you do cast them in a sorry light." Mrs Rhone shook her head.

"It's only the truth, I'm afraid. Still, they finally came around to mother, she had quite a way with her and so I, the unruly sprog of Oscar O'Harris the prodigal brother, paid my first visit to this grand manor in, I think, 1898. I was six and found it all quite horrid. Everything was so old-fashioned and stuffy. Auntie Flo really couldn't abide children, I dare say that was why she never had any! She terrified the living daylights out of me, no surprise I suppose after she whipped me herself for riding down the banister in the grand hall."

The colonel laughed.

"Too tempting that polished wood!"

"Quite right," O'Harris joined in. "But Auntie Flo was a harridan and I only dared it once. Odd, in the end really, how I grew so fond of her, but there you are."

"Money does that to you, old boy!" The colonel, a little too merry for his own good, put caution to the wind.

O'Harris laughed with him, but Clara noted a frown on his forehead. The comment had stung, but was that because it was true or because it was not?

"Anyway, Uncle Goddard was a bit more of a laugh. Even helped me put together the model fort he had had as a boy, he was rather fond of military stuff and could go on for hours and hours about British battles. If we played at soldiers, he always had to be the English and he *always* had to win. Used to bawl my eyes out over it, until my father agreed to play and then we could both be the English and fight him," O'Harris smiled to himself. "You forget that sort of thing, don't you? But he was a good soul, old Goddard. Constantly being harangued by Auntie Flo, of course, some days I thought the old beggar would just curl up into himself like a tortoise and pretend he wasn't there. He looked like someone who could do with a shell to hide inside."

"Florence was a forceful character, but a kind woman at heart," Mrs Rhone objected mildly. "She always donated lovely things to the church raffles."

"I tell it as I saw it Mrs Rhone," O'Harris rebuffed her politely. "Still, I was only six and perhaps that was a bad week I visited. After that I paid a visit most summers, sometimes with the folks, other times alone. Funny how they seemed to age every time I came, like each winter had scoured a little more life from them. Goddard in particular."

"Someone once told me he was quite ill," the colonel remarked. "Could have been my old father actually when I was home on leave. One of those nasty wasting illnesses."

"Nonsense!" Mrs Rhone interrupted. "He was fit as a fiddle!"

"Your uncle and aunt seem to have been masters of contradiction," Clara smiled at O'Harris.

He grinned back.

"Now, I've been rambling on, I do apologise, I must get to the mystery at hand. You see, I was trying to paint a picture of them for you. I know detectives lay a good deal of stock in a person's character and manner when making their case."

"Sometimes," Clara answered noncommittally, she was hoping the expectant crowd were not anticipating a clear-cut, instant solution from her.

"So, let's spin on a decade or two. Last time I saw Uncle Goddard alive was in 1913. I was twenty-one and just finished from university, having utterly failed my maths exams. I was on somewhat of a retreat from life, not really knowing what I was going to do and quite depressed with myself. Remarkably, old Goddard and Flo proved to be sympathetic to my peril. I remember Goddard spending all his time talking with me, trying to fix up my future. I felt quite rotten for messing up everybody's expectations, but Goddard wouldn't let me feel sorry for myself. I'm afraid I blew my top with him a few times, was determined to hate myself and didn't like being told to buck up. Regret it now of course, in fact, regretted it at the time and always meant to apologise, just never got around to it. Then it was October, and I was back off to London to face my seemingly doomed future – though not as bad as I thought in the end – and just over a week later we had the news Goddard was dead.

"Of course, they hid the fact of the missing corpse. They even had a funeral with an empty casket. Quite incredible. I probed Auntie Flo for the details, I was pretty obnoxious about it really, still was carrying around the guilt of not apologising to him before he died, I suppose. Anyway, she told me they had just finished dinner in the dining room as usual, Colonel Brandt, here, was their guest."

"Indeed, I was!" The colonel gave a toast to the air with his glass in agreement.

"And Goddard said he was just going outside for a cigar, Auntie Flo wouldn't let him smoke in the house because she said it stained the wallpaper," O'Harris continued. "Out he trotted, down the terrace steps, between the formal roses and barely a minute passes and, *thump*! They hear him fall and, well, actually the Colonel should tell this bit."

The colonel suddenly looked flustered at being handed the reins of the story but rose to the challenge valiantly.

"As Captain O'Harris said, I was sitting at the dining table having just finished a lovely lamb and onion pie and feeling quite nicely full, I might add, the cook in those days was extraordinary. The lightest of pastry-makers, oh yes! In fact, I remember that pie almost as clearly as the events that followed it. I was just dabbing some gravy from my coat jacket and listening to Florence remarking on the state of the military, not quite up to the standards of when Goddard was an officer, etc, etc, when we heard this thud. Sort of a clatter, then a thud. Like someone stumbling into something and then falling. Well, I look at Florence and she looks at me and then we both jump up and run to the window, and there is old Goddard face down on the path between the roses.

"We ran down the steps towards him and rolled him over. His eyes were popping out his skull and his mouth gaped. There was no doubt he was dead, though I listened for a heartbeat, nonetheless. Florence was shaken, but she was always stoical. Most women would have screamed seeing their dead husband lying on the ground, but she got to her feet and said she would fetch a doctor. She was racing back towards the house before I could tell her there was no point.

"Oh, but the more I looked at wretched Goddard, the more I felt it was all horribly wrong. I know the rumours were that he was ill, perhaps his heart gave out, you might argue, but it was the look on his face. I don't know, there was something there that chilled me. Like that old legend of seeing the face of a murderer reflected in his victim's eyes for a few moments after death. I just knew something awful had happened. I've seen enough dead men in my time, but this, this was different. I just got up and took to my heels to find the nearest policeman. I should have told Florence, really, but I was so flustered."

The colonel shook his head sadly.

"By the time I got back with a policeman the body had just... vanished. Like a magic trick. Florence was crying and couldn't fathom what had happened. The doctor was then turning up too. The policeman was rightly unimpressed by the scene, and it took a lot of talking to persuade him there genuinely had been a body. Of course, not being able to find Goddard alive helped prove that. But the body was gone! Just gone! They searched all over as soon as the dawn came up. Never knew a thing like it, quite remarkable."

Chapter Four

"Miss Fitzgerald, what do you make of it all?" O'Harris leaned over and topped up Clara's sherry glass as he asked.

Clara mused on the question as she took a short sip. She was not a great drinker.

"It is certainly peculiar," she said, hedging her bets as her audience leaned in excitedly. "I am inclined to agree with the Colonel that it was foul play."

"Knew it!" Colonel Brandt laughed jovially.

"But why is that, Miss Fitzgerald?" O'Harris pressed.

"Because the body was moved," Clara said simply. "Assuming the Colonel was correct, and Goddard was dead, and I feel the Colonel a man familiar enough with this subject to not make a simple error, then the only way the body could vanish was if someone else moved it, and the only reason someone would want to move a body is if they had something to hide."

"Like a murder!" The colonel said enthusiastically.

"Or, at least, they felt responsible for Goddard O'Harris' death. That might not imply murder as such, but someone had a guilty conscience that night and it drove them to take a terrible risk and move the body."

"But, where to?" Demanded the colonel. "I mean, the police were there in minutes, hardly time to bury a man!"

"Oh Colonel!" Mrs Rhone said aghast.

Clara ignored her.

"There is no reason to suppose the body was only moved *once*. Initially the person took it somewhere nearby and handy for concealment, then they went back when the coast was clear and moved it somewhere more suitable. You said yourself the police did not begin searching until dawn, that leaves many hours in which to hide a body."

"By Jove, she is a smart lass!" The colonel grinned at O'Harris. "So, my girl, tell me this, who did the deed?"

Clara hesitated.

"What's this? Cat got your tongue?" Brandt asked.

Clara glanced at O'Harris, uncomfortable with the thoughts running through her mind. Then she sighed, there was no getting away from the colonel without an answer.

"I must first state that with the limited facts of this case I can only make a supposition, which, if I was to examine the details further, might prove inaccurate."

"Don't be so coy, girl!"

"Colonel," interrupted O'Harris. "Go on Clara, we appreciate the difficulties."

Clara wondered if he really did but continued anyway.

"We have to ask ourselves who had the motive and the opportunity to kill Goddard, and of course we don't know for certain what actually did kill him. It had to be something fast-acting and, going by the Colonel's brief glance at the body it was probably something internally ingested rather than, let us say, a bullet, which would have left a wound you would have noticed, yes Colonel?"

"Certainly! I know a bullet hole when I see one."

"So that leaves us with few choices, but I would not like to rule anything out unless I was able to have a coroner's view on the matter, which is, similarly, impossible," Clara tried to still the slight shake in her hands as she presented her case as she saw it, the last thing she wanted to do was hurt the charming and handsome Captain O'Harris. "What we can say was that the method used was quick, soundless, or at least very quiet, and instantaneously deadly. That rules out most poisons by the way, even strychnine requires at least half-an-hour to kill someone."

"Clara's last case involved strychnine," Tommy pointed out helpfully.

"Yes, but not as a murder weapon, in fact," Clara added. "Anyway, all that aside, I have to come to the conclusion that whoever killed Goddard O'Harris was near him immediately before his death and that leaves only two suspects."

"By Jove, she means me and Mrs O'Harris," the colonel laughed in astonishment.

"Indeed, I do Colonel, but I am inclined to rule you out as you were the first to run for the police which, I admit, could have been a ploy, but you were also not present to move the body. Also, I do not see your motive, though of course you could easily have one I do not know about, but then there is your keenness on retelling the story. Most murderers would prefer not to discuss their crime, unless they are of an unstable or insane persuasion, in case it draws attention to them."

The colonel let out another rumbling laugh.

"Dear me, this is good fun. I am quite flattered to be considered a suspect but feel it rather depressing how quickly you ruled me out."

"Please Colonel," Mrs Rhone begged piteously. "This is quite appalling."

"Miss Fitzgerald," O'Harris spoke up, "I take this to mean, excluding the Colonel as you have, you believe my aunt killed Uncle Goddard?"

Clara hesitated again, the dashing captain looked hurt and not a little stunned, she was starting to realise that he had genuinely been fond of his aunt.

"I know nothing for certain," Clara insisted. "I just mean that, were we to take this as a theoretical exercise, the most likely candidate for the crime, both because she had the means and the opportunity to kill Goddard, along with being the only person present to be able to move the body while the Colonel was fetching help, was Florence O'Harris."

"Oh no!" Mrs Rhone gasped. "Oh, but it could be, oh…"

"And what of motive?" O'Harris asked rather sharply.

"That I do not know, except that wives often wish to kill their husbands and vice versa, the majority of them simply do not act upon the urge."

"Oh Miss Fitzgerald, what an awful thing to say, I have never wished to kill my husband!" Cried Mrs Rhone.

Clara turned to her seriously.

"Really Mrs Rhone? Not even just once without really meaning it, but just thinking it in anger?"

"Well…" Mrs Rhone glanced over to her husband the vicar who was sound asleep in a chair. "I suppose once, yes, when he sprayed weedkiller instead of insecticide on my prize begonias and ruined them all. It was just a week before the village garden show. I could have killed him, oh yes, my dear, I do see what you mean. We all say it don't we? Just mostly we don't mean it."

"Exactly," Clara said.

"And then there was the time he invited that obnoxious Mrs Vine to tea because she wanted to discuss the jumble sale with me and I had already told him I wanted nothing to do with it after the way I was treated the year before and then I ended up agreeing to it anyway over scones with Mrs Vine," Mrs Rhone was enjoying herself now. "And the time he wore the new gloves I had knitted for him specially to help dig some sheep out of the snow at a neighbouring farm and they came home ruined, and he knows how I hate knitting."

"I think we get the impression, dear lady," Colonel Brandt cast a worried look at the woman. "Quite remarkable the good reverend is still alive."

"This is all nonsense," Captain O'Harris snapped abruptly and left the party to stalk over to a window and gaze out furiously at the evening sky.

Clara groaned inwardly. She had dreaded as much, it seemed a crime was not always best solved, especially one so long in the past and personal to her host.

"Do you think Florence moved the body herself?" Colonel Brandt was oblivious to the fury his game had caused O'Harris.

"It is possible, though I wouldn't rule out an accomplice. I'm afraid that puts you back in the picture Colonel, you may have returned later to help Florence."

"Marvellous!" The colonel roared merrily. "Of course, I do protest my innocence, but it is rather pleasing to think even at my age a young lady could consider me notorious!"

Clara was hardly listening to him; she was staring at captain O'Harris' back and feeling horribly guilty.

The evening party began to break up. Mrs Rhone woke her husband and explained they were going home. Colonel Brandt picked up his walking stick and unsteadily made his way to their host, shaking his hand and thanking him for the food and brandy.

Clara, pushing Tommy in his wheelchair, was the last to go.

"Don't be glum," Tommy said sympathetically, but Clara knew she had ruined the evening, at least for O'Harris.

He joined them at the door to say goodbye.

"Look, I was rather abrupt..." he began.

"I should not have said so much," Clara quickly interrupted. "I should have had more sense. I never was one for tact."

"That is true," Tommy interjected.

"It's just..." O'Harris stared at the high ceiling of the hall, trying to pull together his warring emotions. "I always thought Uncle Goddard was murdered and that it wasn't right how no one was ever caught for the crime. Now you say it might have been Auntie Flo and, well, I stood at that window staring outside and I was furious at your suggestion, but slowly it occurred to me that it could be true. Isn't that awful?"

"Sometimes it is best not to dig up the past," Clara said unhappily. "I didn't mean to pain you."

"No, don't apologise. This is something that has hung over the family for years. If Auntie Flo did it... and if she did not... You see Clara, I just have to know. Now you have begun this I have to know for sure. I wasn't lying when I said I cared about Auntie Flo, I cared a great deal, but we grew to know each other after Goddard died, she seemed... different after that. I assumed it was the shock and grief, now I have to know if it was something else," O'Harris drew a deep breath. "I don't just flee this house every winter because of the cold, you know. These walls hold ghosts, oh not the shrieking, theatrical kind, but memories of those who went before, and I don't always feel comfortable alone here. Maybe that's because of what happened to Goddard, or maybe deep down I have always had my suspicions of my aunt's involvement. In any case, I want to know the truth, whether it is painful or not."

Clara knew what he was about to ask and wished he wouldn't.

"I want you to come back tomorrow and start investigating my uncle's death."

"Captain O'Harris, these old stories, when you delve into them you are bound to dig up secrets and it can be hurtful. No one is perfect, but in our memories loved ones can seem better than they really were and when we scratch at that veneer it can be extremely unpleasant."

"I understand that," O'Harris persisted. "But I want you to investigate for me. I need to know the truth, sometimes living with only half an answer is just as hurtful as knowing the truth."

"And if I discover the worst?"

"I am a grown man, Miss Fitzgerald. I can handle whatever information you uncover." O'Harris looked so forlorn that Clara felt her resolve caving – would it be so bad, after all, to spend a little more time here in the good captain's company?

"I can make no promises for a solution, but I will do what I can."

"I am so glad you agreed," O'Harris said, even raising a smile. "And I will pay for your time, of course, what is your usual rate?"

"Shilling an hour," Tommy interrupted quickly.

Clara wanted to kick him.

"I'll pay you a pound an hour, that seems more than fitting for the service you will be doing me."

"That is too generous..." Clara managed before Tommy pinched her arm.

"I insist, and Mr Fitzgerald you must come tomorrow too and get a good look at the *Buzzard*."

Tommy's face broke into a big grin.

"Thank you, old boy!"

"I know a fellow aviation enthusiast when I see one," O'Harris replied. "Well Miss Fitzgerald?"

"I suppose I shall see you tomorrow," Clara said.

"About 11 o'clock?"

"Yes, that is acceptable."

"Good, I'll send a car for you."

Clara couldn't help her surprise.

"A car?"

Chapter Five

The car was painted burgundy and glistened and sparkled in the morning sunlight. A grey liveried chauffeur opened the door for Clara and refused to let her help him assist Tommy into the vehicle. Sitting in the open-topped car as they whistled down the country lanes Clara experienced a tremor of nerves as she clutched her hat to her head. Other than in a train, she had never travelled so fast.

"Do you suppose he knows what he is doing?" She asked her brother.

"Isn't this grand, old bean!" Tommy said back, the roar of the engine and the wind whisking by obscuring her question. "If only my legs worked Clara! Think of what I could do!"

"Is that a cow ahead?"

They both cried out as the driver whipped them around a corner and confronted a black and white Friesian in the centre of the road. He beeped his horn loudly, barely slowing, and the animal ambled up the grass verge in time to avoid being mown down.

"That was dreadfully dangerous!" Clara gasped.

"Old girl, once everyone learns the rules of the road there won't be a problem."

"Really?" Clara said cynically. "Didn't you read about that road accident in the paper? The man on the bicycle and the Bentley?"

"Yes, yes, but that is all ignorance. Mark my words, once we get the hang of cars there won't be any accidents. You just have to have a little sense, that's all."

"Excuse me if I don't entirely believe you," Clara snorted, wondering who was going to teach road sense to the cows and sheep that dotted the rural fields they flew past.

There was one thing she could not criticise, however. They arrived at Captain O'Harris' house far quicker than they ever could have done on foot. As they pulled into the drive O'Harris waved at them and bounced down the steps to open the car door for Clara.

"My dear, you look rather windswept," he laughed, offering his hand.

"We nearly killed a cow," Clara said indignantly. "And no one informed me I was to travel open air at high speeds."

"The beast can go some," O'Harris grinned, patting his car affectionately. "I call her Speedy Suzy, after an old flame."

"Dare I ask if the girl would be insulted?"

"I imagine she would, Suzy was anything but speedy, but she did look good in dark red."

"Captain O'Harris!" Tommy appeared around the side of the car being pushed by the chauffeur in his wheelchair. "You don't know how I envy you. This car is magnificent! If only I was not confined to this chair."

Tommy deflated slightly as reality sank in.

"Don't get dispirited, I wouldn't have sent it if I thought it would plunge you down in the dumps." O'Harris said quickly.

"It's not that," Tommy glanced longingly at the car. "People don't know what it is to dream of doing the impossible."

"I do," O'Harris assured him. "I dreamt of flying and people laughed, they told me never, they told me give up. But there I was in the war, skimming the skies. Who says one day you won't drive a car or even fly a plane too?"

"The doctors say it," Tommy answered glumly.

"And what do they know?" O'Harris shook his head. "If I believed everything my doctors told me then I shouldn't be standing before you. My doctors tell me my heart's not quite what it should be and could stop at any second from a sudden shock. If they had known that in the flying corps, they would have never let me fly, but I'm not one to listen to that nonsense and here I am as fit as a fiddle!"

"I appreciate the story, but my legs aren't ever going to work again."

"You don't give them a chance with that attitude. If I were you, I would be trying to walk every day and who knows, just maybe, I would manage it if I tried hard enough, but the important thing is not to give up."

"Quite right," Clara interrupted deciding it was time to change the subject and deflect Tommy's thoughts from his legs. "Now, I do believe you have a mystery for me to solve Captain O'Harris?"

"Oh yes, where are my manners! Come in, come in! Would you like tea or coffee?"

They followed him into the house and through into the dining room where they had sat and eaten the day before.

"I thought we should start here," O'Harris explained. "Scene of the crime, well almost. Though, I confess, after sleeping on the matter I wonder if I have sent you on a wild goose chase Miss Fitzgerald."

"Most mysteries look that way at the start, but the answers are usually to be found if you hunt hard enough for them."

"I admire your confidence. Where do we begin?"

Clara had been mulling this moment over in her head since the night before.

"I was wondering at maybe recreating the scene?" She said. "Tommy can be Colonel Brandt. I shall play the part of Aunt Florence and you…"

She tailed off as she realised what she was suggesting.

"I shall be Uncle Goddard. Do not be perturbed Miss Fitzgerald, I am not morbid, and it is quite logical I should play the role. Shall we sit at the table?"

"Yes, but… ah, is the table in the same place it was back then?"

O'Harris stared at the table for a long moment.

"Now you mention it, I believe it was more to the right. Yes, yes, we moved it when the new sideboard came to make it more convenient for serving, but it was indeed a good two foot further towards the far wall."

"Meaning the Colonel could have had a clear view of Goddard walking down the terrace steps." Clara moved across the room, assessing how the bars of the windows and the heavy stone balustrade of the terrace obscured the view.

"Is it important?" O'Harris asked.

"Well, that's just the thing. I can never be sure if it is or isn't until I rule it out."

"Do you want to move the table?" O'Harris glanced at the heavy mahogany dining table, decorated with an elaborate floral centrepiece and candlesticks. "I'd have to call a servant."

"No, let us just move the chairs."

Clara took a chair, as did O'Harris and Tommy carefully wheeled himself into place.

"Now we have an issue." Tommy said, "We don't know where they all sat."

"Uncle Goddard would have been at the head of the table." O'Harris motioned to the space where his uncle's chair would have been, "We can assume Colonel Brandt and my aunt sat opposite each other either side of him, that was the usual arrangement."

"So, here, maybe?" Tommy wheeled himself into a position roughly in the middle of the imaginary table.

"Not so far down, my uncle hated having his guests at a distance. He was getting deaf, and it meant he had trouble following the conversation. No, they would have been right next to him."

Tommy re-positioned his wheelchair to one side of the head of the table. Clara sat opposite him. O'Harris was last to take his place.

"Right, we have had our supper, and we are contemplating a glass of brandy, or at least the Colonel is," said Clara. "Goddard is thinking about his cigar."

The captain, suddenly getting into the swing of the action, pretended to produce a cigar case and remove one.

"I say Florence, I think I will have my evening cigar," he said, lifting his voice and flattening his accent.

"Not inside Goddard, you know how it discolours the wallpapers," Clara said in her best disapproving voice.

O'Harris got up and walked to the terrace windows. Without looking Clara heard him open them and his steps descend.

"We should be talking politely," she remarked to her brother. "How much can you see, by the way?"

"From here I can see directly down the terrace steps, ah, yes, O'Harris has paused between the rose bushes and is pretending to smoke. I say, he has quite gotten into the part."

Clara raised an eyebrow, in her experience men were rather fond of theatricals and enjoyed any excuse to show off.

"Oh, right, he has now tumbled to the ground."

"Did you hear anything?" Clara asked.

Tommy paused.

"I'm not sure, because I was looking, well... I couldn't say."

"I can't say I heard anything," Clara got to her feet and went to the open terrace doors to call to O'Harris. "Could you do that again? We want to hear the noise you make when you fall."

"Right-oh," waved O'Harris.

Clara returned to her seat.

"This time do not watch him Tommy but focus on me."

"Then how shall I know he has fallen?"

"How indeed," nodded Clara. "The problem is the participants in this mystery are either dead or have lived so much life beyond this adventure that recalling its particulars is rather hard."

"You think the Colonel didn't tell the whole truth?"

"I think he told what he remembered of the event, but the mind is very good at filling in blanks, such as the sound of someone falling."

"Yes, but if that is the case, how did they know he had collapsed?"

"Exactly."

"I say chaps, are you done, I've been lying on that grass a good few minutes and no one came."

They both turned around to look at O'Harris.

"We didn't hear you," apologised Clara. "Could you try again."

Looking slightly forlorn O'Harris returned outside to the garden.

"Supposing they didn't hear him, suppose that filtered into the Colonel's imagination later, that means poor Goddard could have been dead on the ground for ages." Tommy continued where they had left off.

"It raises more possibilities than that, for instance did the Colonel do what you did and watch Goddard without thinking and see him fall, then over time his memory faded to him *imagining* he heard the fall rather than seeing it. That is quite an innocent explanation."

"You think there are non-innocent ones?"

"Oh, there are always non-innocent explanations, but that doesn't mean they are the correct ones. Do you suppose he has dropped yet?"

"I didn't hear anything."

"Let's listen in silence, I feel quite mean making him keep tumbling down on that hard ground."

They fell quiet and listened, after several moments had passed footsteps were heard on the stone terrace steps.

"The gardener just stumbled over me," O'Harris said sheepishly, appearing in the doorway. "He was quite concerned, and it took some explaining, I tell you, to convince him I was fine and just trying out a theory. Did you hear me that time?"

"Sorry, not a peep," Clara came to him and looked him over. "Now what did the Colonel say? Something about the noise."

"He said there was a clatter and a thud like someone had stumbled into something," Tommy answered helpfully.

"There is nothing but rosebushes to stumble into down there," O'Harris remarked. "And they definitely don't clatter."

"Could Goddard have been wearing something that made a lot of noise when he fell?" Asked Clara.

O'Harris paused in thought for a moment.

"I really can't think of anything, wasn't as though he was the mayor and went about wearing his ceremonial chains."

"That raises problem number one, then," Clara walked to the open terrace door and stared into the garden. "Colonel Brandt and Florence O'Harris could not have heard Goddard fall to the ground, so how did they know he had collapsed?"

"That sounds rather suspicious," O'Harris looked uncomfortable.

"Don't worry old boy, just as likely Clara will find a reasonable explanation for it," Tommy assured him.

"Oh yes," added Clara. "It just needs clearing up, but no need to consider it sinister."

"So, is that the end of our dinner party?" Tommy asked.

"For the moment. I'm off to look at the rose beds and then explore the garden for likely body burial spots. Think you two chaps can keep yourselves amused while I am gone?"

O'Harris glanced at Tommy.

"Sounds like we are surplus to requirements," he said.

"It's often like that," Tommy answered.

"I do believe I promised you a look at old *Buzzard*?"

"That you did," grinned Tommy.

"I keep her up in an old, converted barn, I'll escort you there now. That all right Clara?"

They glanced up to see Clara had vanished out onto the terrace.

Chapter Six

The rose bushes were a dead end. Clara saw that straight away; it was over a decade since the murder had occurred and whatever had been there that night was long gone. She still made a brief search of the spot for the sake of thoroughness, examining a few early rose buds that were just beginning to open.

"That's *Parson's Pink China*," a voice remarked behind her.

Clara turned and spotted a gardener in his dirt-covered overalls watching her.

"I'm afraid you have me at a loss when it comes to roses."

"It's an old Chinese rose, so I am told. Perhaps them Orientals call it something different in their gardens, do you think?"

"I imagine they do," Clara smiled. "These bushes are well-grown and look very healthy, have they been here long?"

"Some of them were here in my father's day, if you take care of a rose, it can last a lifetime, especially the old varieties. Those modern ones are different, they are just a flash in the pan and then they die. Like so many modern things. Can't beat an old rose for toughness, I say."

"I would quite like a rose bush in my garden, but they do require some care, do they not?" Clara asked, drawing the man closer.

He huffed.

"Those that know 'em wouldn't say such. It's just no one has any time these days and they think of pruning or spraying a plant as time-consuming and not worth it. They would rather buy them colourful pansies that do as they please for a year and then rot away. All a rose needs is a little care and attention and it will reward you, look here." The gardener lifted up a sprig of a rose bush gently and motioned to the recently trimmed stems, "I come out every morning and trim 'em a little, better than a sharp attack all in one go. It's just like a morning shave, I take off any diseased leaves and burn 'em and I trim any branches that are straying from the bush, and I am rewarded by these bright little buds, all ready to bloom for me. Can't say a rose don't show its gratitude for a touch of love."

"Indeed, you cannot," Clara agreed. "You are very knowledgeable. I take it you have tended the roses here for many years?"

"Oh yes, since my father come here in, what would it be? Summer of 1875. I would have been 14 or 15 then and I helped him about the gardens. Old gardener had died of apoplexy winter before, and the family had let the plants go to wrack and ruin while they decided to find a new man. Quite lucky they were to get my father, I might add. Queen Victoria considered him herself, but he had an aversion to dogs which caused them some difficulties, so he was never offered the position."

"You were here when Mr Goddard O'Harris was alive?"

"Indeed, I was. Funny thing..." he hesitated.

"What is it? I hope I have not upset you?"

"Don't be silly missus, I'm only the gardener, you haven't got to fuss yourself worrying about upsetting me. It's just a few moments ago I came across the young master lying prone on this very spot, and it took me queer because of the remembering."

"Remembering?

"Yes, of poor Mr Goddard and how he was found lying just here," the gardener had seemed to have gone very pale and leaned without thinking against his precious roses.

"I do apologise for my ignorance, I was unaware that any tragedy had befallen the O'Harris family," Clara lied sweetly. "But you look rather pale, shall we take a walk and perhaps that will refresh you?"

"Thank you, missus, most kind, most kind. I left my barrow over by the French Marigolds I was setting, perhaps we can walk that way?"

"Of course!"

They ambled along quietly, Clara waiting with infinite patience to see if her new informant would start talking again, she was not disappointed.

"I don't usually get so spooked, like," the gardener looked abashed. "I am a rational man and I know spirits don't come back, but just for a moment when I saw Captain O'Harris lying there it was like I was going back almost ten years to that awful night."

"I'm terribly sorry, what a shock it must have been to see the body of your employer lying among the roses."

"Oh, it was a dreadful night. Mr Goddard always smoked a cigar among the roses, I would have liked to have complained to him about the harm it caused them, but what is a gardener to do?"

Clara nodded sympathetically.

"On that night I was late out because the old compost heap had rotted through its wooden panels and collapsed all over cook's winter lettuces. I was trying to fix it and it had taken such a time. I was walking back to my little cottage by lamplight, quite rightly I ain't supposed to wander through the gardens in the evening in case people are dining and see me go by, but I was too tired to worry and the only soul about was usually just Mr Goddard and he was a kind-hearted fellow," the gardener fingered at the handle of his barrow. "I think that is why it took me hard seeing him lying there on the ground. Then I looked up from the body, stunned of course, and I see Mrs O'Harris standing on the steps of the terrace with a shawl about her. 'It's all right Mr Riggs, I've sent for the doctor,' she said, calm as anything, she was always a remarkable woman."

Clara's mind pinged at the information. Aunt Florence had gone back to the body after calling for a doctor and it had still been there! That was a different story to the one the colonel had told and rested suspicion once again on Mrs O'Harris. What a shame for the captain.

"Mrs O'Harris must have been dreadfully upset."

"She was a strong woman, some say hard, but I seen her cry over the death of her best magnolia. Person who can weep for the death of a plant can't be bad in my book."

"You stayed with her until the police arrived?"

"Oh no!" The gardener was shocked. "What an imposition that would have been! No, I went home and went to bed. I had a hedge to trim back in the morning."

"Thank you, Mr Riggs, I do apologise for interfering with your work."

"No harm done, Missus. I like to talk about the roses."

Clara was moving off, smiling at him.

"*Parson's China Rose*, was it?"

"*Parson's Pink China*," Mr Riggs called out. "And they like a bit of sun but not too much."

Clara waved to him as she headed across the lawn.

The plane roared throatily as it sailed through the clouds.

"This is the life!" Captain O'Harris called back to his passenger.

"I've never felt so free!" Replied Tommy, staring over the side of the plane down at the tiny houses and gardens.

He felt like a giant stalking over a toy town, the world spread out in a map beneath him.

"What was it like, flying in the war?"

"Bloody terrifying!" O'Harris laughed. "But don't tell a soul I said that Tommy, it's just a secret between us war veterans."

"Quite right," Tommy promised.

"It was Hell being a spotter pilot, flying over No Man's Land, dodging whatever the Germans tried to throw at you. Don't get me wrong, most of their gear couldn't reach us, but they were working on anti-aircraft weapons, and you never knew when the next machine gun you heard was going to be the one with enough long-range on it to hit you. Then there were the other fellows in their planes. They would swarm all over you and all the chap behind you had was a Thompson rifle to try and shoot them!"

"Sounds about as well-organised as us sloggers on the ground!"

"Ah, Tommy, you don't know how I felt for you sods as I flew over. Sometimes we were so low we could see the bodies and then the ones who were hurt but still alive and calling for help. The times I wished I could do something..."

"Didn't we all?" Interrupted Tommy. "I found the only way to deal with it was not to think about the poor souls left out there."

"What happened to you? If you don't mind me asking."

"I used to mind, but you have to get past it. I was machine gunned and left for dead in the mud of No Man's Land."

O'Harris grimaced.

"That's grim, for all I know you were one of the fellows I flew over and wished I could help. I reported every man I saw you know, every single one."

"Don't beat yourself up, old boy. We all had a job to do."

O'Harris banked the plane over, circling around his estate.

"I wanted to fly as long as I can remember," he said as they soared over his home. "Even before I knew such things as planes existed. Does it sound awfully morbid if I say I would rather die in a plane than grow old and wither away?"

"A little," Tommy admitted. "But I am certain most people think similar things."

"And you?"

Tommy hesitated, then a sad smile lit his face.

"Maybe before the war, but after it, all I could think of was living as long as possible."

O'Harris swooped temptingly low over a chimney and Tommy almost reached out his hand to touch the top.

"I say, isn't that your sister by the barn?"

"Don't say so, old boy, it means the game is up!"

O'Harris laughed.

"The poor *Buzzard* is low on fuel, anyway, shall we treat your sister to a first-class landing?"

"Don't expect her to be impressed. Clara doesn't believe in being impressed by people."

O'Harris laughed again and brought the *Buzzard* around to land on the grassy strip outside the converted barn.

"Hold tight!"

The *Buzzard's* rubber wheels hit the ground with a bump, and she coasted along a few yards before her tail sank down and her tail wheel bounced on the grass. The *Buzzard* rolled several more feet, her noisy engine and propeller seeming to make a cacophony of noise within the surrounding trees. Slowly the *Buzzard* came to a halt and O'Harris cut the engine. Her polished wooden propeller finished one last rotation and fell still. The *Buzzard* was at a standstill, but to Tommy she still seemed to hum with life and energy.

"Tommy Fitzgerald!" Clara was running up to them looking furious. "What are you doing?"

"Calm down, dear sister. I was trying out the *Buzzard* for size," Tommy grinned at her.

"My fault, I fear, Miss Fitzgerald. I lured him in. The *Buzzard* likes a run every day, you know, and company makes a flight that much more fun."

"These contraptions are dangerous!" Clara snapped.

For the first time Tommy noticed how pale she had gone.

"I'm fine Clara, honestly."

Clara bit at her lip, controlling her anxiety. She had warned herself about being a nag as she stood by the barn and watched the plane descend, but she couldn't help the churning sensation in her stomach every second the *Buzzard* had remained in the air. Tommy was the last remnant of her family and the loss of him would be too much to bear.

"Have you been busy?" Tommy tried changing the subject.

"Just wandering around the grounds," Clara released the breath she had unknowingly been holding. "I met the gardener."

"Any new information?" O'Harris asked hopefully.

Clara just shook her head, not wanting to tell him that what she had learned seemed to point the finger of blame firmly at his aunt.

"That's a pity, but I suppose it was to be expected," O'Harris jumped from the plane and moved around to manhandle Tommy out of the passenger seat. It was quite a procedure. The back cockpit was high up and Tommy had no means of helping and had to rely on the strength of his host. He felt a hot fury burning inside him as he clung to O'Harris helplessly.

"The wheelchair is in the barn," the captain told Clara.

She nodded mutely and went to fetch it. Several more moments of pulling and dragging succeeded in getting Tommy out of the cockpit and O'Harris perched him on the wing of the plane.

"I hate this," Tommy grumbled.

"Being helped?"

"Being helpless."

O'Harris shrugged.

"What can you do about it?"

Clara reappeared with the wheelchair.

"When was your hangar built captain?"

O'Harris glanced up at the surprise question.

"The barn?"

"Odd place for a barn, right near the house?"

"Uncle Goddard planned it as a garage, he had a fondness for cars. His are still all in there, at the back under oilcloths. We always called it 'the barn' because it was so tall and, well, it rather looks like a barn."

"When was it built?" Clara repeated.

O'Harris leaned against the tail of the *Buzzard* and contemplated his hangar.

"The foundations were just going in the last time I was here visiting, before Goddard's death."

"Your aunt completed the project then?"

"Yes," O'Harris hesitated again. "Are you thinking that is odd?"

"Not if she cared deeply for your uncle, she may have considered it proper to finish his last project."

A smile came to O'Harris' face.

"You make me feel better. I've been worrying silly about Auntie Flo being a murderess. Come on, time for some lunch I reckon."

O'Harris marched ahead to chase up some lunch, calling to his guests to meet him in the garden room. Clara pushed Tommy away from the plane.

"There could be another reason she finished the barn," Tommy said quietly as their host went out of sight.

"I know," Clara sighed. "She may have done it to hide the body she dumped in the foundations."

Chapter Seven

The garden room was optimistically named as it faced North onto the drive, and the only glimpse of true garden was the edge of some trees and a hint of grass in the distance. Big windows drew in the faint sunshine, though most of the room was cast in shade and chilly. The walls were lined with prints and books, a heavy desk squeezed between two bookcases and a large leather sofa squatted in the centre of the room.

Clara found her natural curiosity taking her over to the desk, which she touched lightly, gently pulling the handle to confirm it was locked.

"In another life I could imagine you a spy or thief, old girl," Tommy grinned at her.

"A spy maybe," Clara shrugged. "But I am not sure I would care for the danger."

Captain O'Harris appeared in the doorway with a bottle of whisky in one hand and Indian tonic water in the other. Behind him a maid came with a tray of glasses.

"Bit of a dismal room, isn't it?" O'Harris gave a sniff at his garden room. "I only brought you here because this is all that remains of my uncle's study. The drawing room used to be his study, but after his death Auntie Flo moved everything she could into here and sold the rest. This is as close as you can come to meeting my uncle in the flesh. Goddard lived for his books and work and sometimes I think I can feel him in here among the old pages. Whisky?"

Clara declined, but Tommy agreed and accepted his glass with relish.

"What did your uncle study?" Clara peered at a print on the wall that appeared to depict a Roman scene with ladies in skimpy clothes and men in togas.

"Military history mostly. He wrote a few books on the subject, nothing particularly spectacular," O'Harris went to a shelf and took off several green bound volumes. "Self-published, I'm afraid. Couldn't find anyone to take him seriously, would you like to read them?"

"Yes, I feel I need to know more about Goddard O'Harris," Clara took the volumes and glanced at the titles. "He was interested in ancient history?"

"Only when it came to military tactics. I did think he wrote a nice piece on the ancient Egyptians' use of chariots in battle. He deserved a little more attention."

Clara put the books on a side table and took another look at the shelves. As O'Harris had mentioned they seemed filled with military titles, everything from the Battle of Hastings to the Crimea. She found herself wondering what a man so intimate with ancient warfare would have thought of the Great War.

"Can you open the desk?"

O'Harris rooted a bunch of keys from his pocket. They hung on a wide ring, dozens of them, some small, some large, a few so tarnished they could hardly have been used in years.

"It's one of these," he said bashfully. "You would be amazed how many keys a house like this can acquire. I haven't opened his desk in years. It was mostly full of old business papers and house deeds."

O'Harris finally found a key he seemed to like and walked to the desk and unlocked the front. Clara came forward and started opening drawers and examining contents.

"Looking for anything in particular?" O'Harris asked with a note of anxiety.

"Motive," Clara smiled at him. "So far I can't see a single reason anyone would want your uncle dead."

"Even Auntie Flo?" O'Harris asked keenly.

"Even Aunt Florence, but that isn't to say I am convinced she is in the clear," Clara pulled out some papers and examined them. "Did he make a will?"

"Oh, Uncle Goddard had one for years," O'Harris nodded. "I have it in a safe. He left everything to Auntie Flo. I think there was a little placed aside for some charity, let me think, veterans of war perhaps? I didn't get a penny, which, I must admit, was a shock to the system. I didn't expect money of course, and I did not think of Goddard as my way into the family fortune, but I suppose it hurt a little to think he had left me out of the thing."

Clara flicked through a sheaf of notes on Roman battle tactics.

"Did he leave any debts?"

"Not that I am aware of. He was quite a frugal soul. Aside from the cars, in that way we were very similar. We had a feel for engines and mechanical power, only his was decidedly more on the grounded side."

"What would he make of your record attempt?" Tommy interrupted.

Captain O'Harris leaned back in a chair and took a long sip of whisky.

"I fear he would have been appalled. He hated travel and he was not a man for anything dangerous. He hardly drove his cars, you know, he liked firing them up, hearing the engine purr, but take him on a long drive and he was a nervous wreck. He always thought something awful would happen."

"People get like that as they age."

"He was always old to me," O'Harris smiled fondly at the memory. "He always seemed a little on the ancient side with his books and glasses and his punctual meals."

O'Harris laughed.

"He would never eat after nine o'clock at night because he insisted it affected his liver."

Clara moved away from the desk and took a seat near the dashing captain.

"It sounds as though you were really fond of him."

"I was," O'Harris leaned towards her. "In a way. He was the only adult I knew growing up who talked to me like an equal. He didn't patronise me or instantly explain things. If I didn't understand I had to ask. I always appreciated that. When I was a child, maybe it was the same for you, I always felt very left out. That the adult world was something being kept secret from me, and I was always trying to find my way into it, as if it was a foreign land. School only made me feel more left out, it was us boys against the adults then, it was a funny way to live."

O'Harris took a long look into Clara's eyes. He saw himself faintly reflected in her dark pupils.

"I am not one to be sentimental."

"Nor am I," Clara agreed.

"But these last few days I have found my mind turning back to those long past times and turning over every minute, every hour, perhaps for some clue, but more often just because I can. I've always felt rather lonely," O'Harris paused. "You have been a real breath of fresh air these last two days Clara. It is quite remarkable."

"Should I leave you two alone?" Tommy spoke from behind them.

"I am being a bore, aren't I old boy?" O'Harris laughed. "I'm sure lunch must be ready by now. Let's leave the past and think about today for a while."

He looked to Clara, but she could find nothing to say.

Clara and Tommy arrived home in the late afternoon. Annie was awaiting them with a joint of meat roasting in the oven. She remarked about the fine weather as she hustled them indoors and talked about the local gossip, but Clara only half heard her. She was musing over her day with O'Harris and her thoughts on the case.

After dinner she excused herself and leafed through the Brighton directory to find the address of Colonel Brandt. His name was listed along with a phone number, which she rang only to be told by a servant that he was at his club for the evening. Gaining directions, Clara set out to find the good colonel and try to resolve a piece of the mystery.

Brighton Gentleman's Club could not compete with similar organisations in places such as London, but in its own humble way it provided a retreat from the outside world for those who could afford it and, of course, who were male.

Clara entered the foyer a little uncomfortably. This was almost uncharted territory, though she had heard the local suffragist movement had once staged a march into the building protesting the chauvinistic and isolationist nature of the facility. The club butler glanced up at her as she entered, and it was not a glance that echoed approval.

On the other hand, Clara *was* a twentieth century woman, and she had every right to walk into any building, she told herself. There was no law to deny her the right to step into a Gentleman's Club, it was only tradition and conservative attitudes that made her feel guilty now. She tried to hold her head high and walk confidently as she approached the desk.

"I must urgently speak with Colonel Brandt, and I was informed he was here," she told the butler with her best formal tone.

The butler glared down his nose at her.

"You are aware of where you are?"

"Yes," Clara said calmly. "Now will you please inform the Colonel Miss Clara Fitzgerald is here to see him?"

"That is not our policy," the butler said smoothly. "The Club is supposed to be an escape from the real world and its worries."

He did not quite risk saying it was an escape from women, but Clara knew he was thinking it.

"If I was to tell you the Colonel's cousin had passed away and I needed to inform him about the matter, would you go find him?"

"That is a different situation. It would be reprehensible not to contact him immediately."

"Very well then," Clara nodded. "Please find the Colonel."

The butler looked fazed. Clara waited a moment, then added;

"Well? Go on then?"

The butler, still somewhat bemused, left his post and went in search of Colonel Brandt. A few minutes later both men returned, the colonel grinning.

"Miss Fitzgerald! A pleasure to see you again."

"Colonel," Clara offered her hand for the colonel to shake.

"Very modern," he laughed. "Shall we slip into the guests' parlour? It is the only place women are allowed."

"That would be agreeable. I have things I must talk to you about."

"Yes, my poor late cousin," Colonel Brandt winked mischievously.

He led them to a small side room furnished as a cosy sitting room, with large red leather sofas and a copiously stocked drinks cabinet.

"I was quite bemused when the butler brought me your message. I don't have a cousin," the colonel said.

"I never said you did, nor did I say he died, I am afraid the poor man just made his own assumptions."

Brandt chuckled.

"You are a regular modern woman, Miss Fitzgerald. Can I offer you a drink?"

"Just some tonic water, please."

"So, I suppose this is about the O'Harris business?" Brandt poured her a glass of water while helping himself to a large brandy.

"It is indeed. Do you have any objections to talking about it?"

"I hardly see why," the colonel shrugged. "After all, I started the whole debate, can't hardly back out now, can I?"

He handed Clara her glass.

"Do you still think Flo did it? I really must protest that assumption, it is quite awful. She was a good woman, Miss Fitzgerald. She would never have killed someone."

"Even her husband?"

Colonel Brandt smirked.

"An age-old question, yes wives are always saying they will kill their husbands, aren't they? Truth is, I always thought the pair were quite in love, for all the quarrelling and coldness. But then I never married, so perhaps I can't tell?

The colonel lowered himself into a chair, suddenly looking weary.

"I think that a shame, now I am old. Living in your own company seems marvellous as a young man, but you get to a certain age and so do your friends and suddenly the thought of a lifelong companion seems very appealing."

"Florence filled the void for a time, though?"

The colonel smiled softly.

"She wasn't so much older than me, and yes, I did enjoy her company. She appreciated how it felt being home with no family around me. My father had died by then. Flo always did have a soft spot for a waif and stray."

"And how did you feel about Goddard?"

"Good chap, I told you how his tales of the Boer war made me join the army."

"Were you friends?"

Brandt considered.

"I think that is rather hard to say. We talked a good deal, but we never drank together. Goddard could be a touch aloof. Never joined a club, never was involved in any society, quite kept himself to himself. He used to ask me to dine, though as far as I can tell I was one of the privileged few who were entertained by the O'Harries. A couple who were content in their own company, I suppose."

"Did he have an argument with anyone."

The colonel swirled the drink in his glass.

"Goddard was not the sort to make enemies. I mean, you know the sort of man who turns the world against him, like that butler fellow out front. Ask me if he has enemies and I could list a few, some of them members here. But they aren't the sort who get themselves killed, are they? It's always the fellows who everyone says were well-liked, popular, and quite harmless. Goddard was that sort."

"Even the harmless sort of fellow can upset people. A servant maybe?"

"No, no, Goddard never argued with his servants, that was Flo's job," Brandt laughed and then fell silent. "I'm helping to make your case against her, aren't I?"

"Not really," Clara assured him, though in truth he was, but she didn't want to alert him to the fact. "Do you recall a gardener, Mr Riggs?"

Brandt sank into thought for a while.

"No, can't say I do."

"No matter, it was just a thought. Now tell me a little more about Florence O'Harris."

"What can I say? She was a rather stern person, but deep down she was kind and thoughtful. Look, she was not the sort to murder a person."

"You and I can both agree I am limited as to suspects."

"Yes, and if I could persuade you that I had killed Goddard I would, whether I thought Flo guilty or not. I don't want to see her reputation tainted."

"This investigation is only for the benefit of Captain O'Harris. No one else will ever know a thing."

The colonel rubbed at his balding head, looking strained and worried.

"I've always wondered about Goddard's death. It has troubled me these last years. Even during the war, some nights in the trenches when the other boys were worrying about rats, or dysentery or Hun shells flying over, I was lying on my blanket thinking about Goddard. The night he died is crystal clear in my mind. I can replay every second perfectly."

"Then you can answer another of my questions," Clara continued. "Where were you seated on that night?"

"On the far side of the table, facing Flo and the garden doors. Why?"

"I've been conducting an experiment," Clara said carefully. "You said you heard Goddard fall, yes?"

"Yes?"

"Perhaps it was a still night, for try as hard as I could, I could not hear Captain O'Harris fall in the same place with the doors open."

The colonel hesitated, he visibly paled. For a second his hand shook and the ice in his glass rattled.

"I could have sworn..."

"Years pass and our memories become a little uncertain," Clara reassured him, but the good colonel looked troubled.

"I thought I heard him, all these years I thought... How else could it have been?"

"Perhaps you saw something from the window? Or did Florence mention something?"

The colonel was glancing around the room, trying to muster his thoughts.

"Did I see something?" He mumbled to himself. He shut his eyes and tried to think. "That night, clear as a bell I could picture it. I sat with Flo, she talked I listened, there was a good claret on the table, and I was helping myself when..." the colonel's eyes shot open. "We heard the big clock in the hall chime the hour, 9 o'clock, and Flo glanced at me and then twisted around to look out the windows, but it was dark, too dark to see, and she said, 'Where has that silly husband of mine got to?' Then I stood up and walked to the window and saw him."

The colonel shook his head.

"All these years... but it wasn't Goddard falling but the chiming of the clock that made us look up."

Chapter Eight

Clara reached out and patted his hand.

"Memory is a tricky thing."

"Does this affect your case?"

"I'm not sure, except now I know Goddard O'Harris was dead longer than I had first thought. Probably several minutes elapsed between the time he fell and the time you found him. But whether that means anything I don't know."

"It's a horrible thing, to think you know something and then to have it pointed out you were wrong."

"I am sorry."

"Do not be, you can't spare an old man's feelings in a case like this," the colonel sank back in the chair. "It's too much time mulling over it, I suppose. Too many hours alone to think over it again and again. I'm no use to you, am I? A silly old man."

"Please do not say that," Clara insisted. "There is nothing silly about you, it was a mistake and I pity the man who thinks he never has or never will make one of those."

A smile returned to the colonel's lips.

"Even if you have to prove Flo did this terrible thing, it will be good to get the matter dealt with. Goddard deserves a little justice."

"I would appreciate some additional suspects if you would like to offer any?"

The colonel took the matter into consideration, then there was the familiar shake of the head.

"I'm a bit hopeless, sorry."

"No apologies necessary Colonel. I shall let you get back to your friends."

The colonel shrugged.

"'Friends' is a relative term, Miss Fitzgerald. Since Flo passed, I don't think I have any, really."

"That's a shame," Clara paused at the door of the room. "I hope you are mistaken."

She waved goodbye and then marched out of the club, astutely ignoring the scowling butler.

Back home Clara was greeted by a worried looking Annie.

"Where did you vanish to?" The maid snapped and Clara almost had to laugh, her relationship with the small and sprightly girl was anything but orthodox.

"I had a little business to deal with, oh but Annie, is there any chance of hot cocoa?"

Annie folded her arms across her chest and stood stoutly before her mistress.

"Don't go changing the subject, had me all at sixes and sevens wondering where you were."

"Was Tommy worried?"

"He fell asleep in the armchair right after dinner, didn't even know you were gone. Right fine man-of-the-house he is. Now where did you go?"

"To a gentleman's club."

"Don't be pulling my leg."

"I did Annie, and please do not point at me. I went to see Colonel Brandt who is one of the witnesses in my current case."

"And could it not have waited until morning?"

Clara gave Annie a long look.

"No," sighed the maid. "Course it couldn't."

"If it satisfies you Annie, I feel no further forward for my evening expedition."

"Just in future, would you mind remarking where you are going?" Annie relaxed. "Come on then, I'll see if I can rustle up some cocoa from the pantry."

Clara followed Annie into the kitchen of her home. The Fitzgeralds had been reasonably well-off, and the house had once been thriving with servants. The kitchen remained a testament to those old days when Mr Fitzgerald had been alive and working tirelessly as a lecturer on medical science. The room still had all its pine and oak units, big dressers stacked with copper pots and delicately painted plates, a huge butler sink with an old-fashioned pump standing over it and a massive range that helped warm the house too. And then there was the large oak table in the centre of the room. So well-scrubbed it was almost white, and grazed with countless scratches from pots, plates, and knives.

Clara loved that table. She could recall how cook had stood with her arms up to the elbows in flour kneading bread and pastry and letting Clara help. She had fond memories of Christmas cake mixes being stirred by each household member (for luck) on that table, and rows of jam tarts and gingerbread men being prepared for the local fete. Cook had left them just before the war. Her son signed up and her daughter-in-law nearly broke down in the High Street in distress, so cook went to keep her company. Her son was killed a year later. The male servants of the house also left to join up or help out in other ways if they were too old for military service. By the time Clara's parents were killed the house was running on three maids, one of which doubled as an adequate cook. Clara dismissed them from financial considerations not long after. For almost three years Clara rattled about the house on her own and then Tommy came home a physical and mental wreck and Annie entered her life as a desperately needed helper. She had never looked back, but, just for a moment as she sat at the table, the memories of those old years before the war washed over her. Bittersweet, but still her memories.

"I have a speck or two of cocoa left," Annie grunted, opening a tin canister that had probably not been refilled in four or five years. "It will be mostly milk, or I could stir in some Bovril?"

"No, indeed, I think I shall stick with hot milk and a hint of cocoa."

Annie set the milk in a pan and began carefully bringing it to the verge of boiling.

"You would think by now they could have the shops properly stocked," she moaned. "It's been two years since the war, but Mr Higgins never has any cocoa, nor oranges. I used to love the occasional orange; I would save up for one."

"At least we have the essentials of life; butter, milk, cheese, eggs, and meat no longer exist on a first come first served basis. I missed butter during the war."

"My mam kept a goat. On a good day she could save enough milk to churn. Oh, it didn't always go right, sometimes I would come home and find her crying over a lumpy mess that weren't butter, weren't cheese and certainly weren't edible. But when she did do it right, she could make a reasonable butter. She was quite proud of herself."

"And quite rightly Annie, who, these days, have the skills to churn butter, or even know how?"

"Mam came from farm stock. That goat was our saviour during those first years of the war," Annie slipped into silence, her family had been killed in a bombardment. "Never did find out what happened to old Penny, probably she ran off and someone ate her. That's a bitter thought, isn't it?"

"Don't dwell on it," Clara said.

The milk boiled and Annie poured it into two teacups she had warming on the range. She added a little dash of sugar and then brought them to the table.

"Now, what is this new case that is troubling you? Tommy has given me the gist of it, and it seems quite simple. The woman killed her husband."

"Nothing's simple Annie. Why, is my first question? Then, how? Besides, I don't feel right accusing someone who cannot defend themselves without a little more proof."

"What sort of proof?"

Clara shrugged.

"A written confession would be nice. Annie, have you ever heard anything about the O'Harrises?"

Annie pondered the question.

"Would that be Florence O'Harris?"

"Yes."

"She died a year or two back. Just made the end of the war, I think," Annie sipped her milk. "Now, if I remember rightly, she was rather a fanatical fundraiser for charity and during the war was one of those ladies who collected handmade blankets for the soldiers and had you give her your old scrap iron for the war effort. In fact, I believe she ran several events to raise money for a plane. It was donated to the RFC, and I recall they printed something in the paper?"

"I remember that," Clara nodded. "The Brighton Biplane. I believe it crashed on its first flight?"

"Mrs O'Harris would have not been impressed," Annie smiled. "Oh, she was a fierce one. Chaired so many ladies' committees my mam just called her 'The Chairwoman,' never told you which organisation she meant because she didn't need to, Florence O'Harris was on them all!"

"She wasn't popular then?"

"Yes and no. She was the sort of lady who got things done, but she didn't let anyone else really help and sometimes she was a touch overbearing. Mam always said it was because she was lonely. When did her husband die?"

"1913."

"Then I was only a child," Annie nodded. "I hear she had a garden party every summer at her house, open to the public, but I never went. What about you?"

"My father always took us on holidays during the summer when he wasn't needed for lecturing."

"My mam always said I didn't have a nice enough dress to go, but my dad used to whisper to me, when he saw I was disappointed, it was really because she didn't want to face Mrs O'Harris. I think they clashed a lot."

"I don't suppose she was the only one who clashed with Florence. What about servants? Could she have been a harridan at home too?"

"Wouldn't surprise. Struck me she was the sort of woman who would prefer to run a house herself and saw a housekeeper as an imposition."

"Could revenge against Florence be at the heart of this?"

"Are you thinking a servant?"

Clara gave a sigh, which rapidly turned into a yawn.

"It is just another of my random thoughts. The trouble is Goddard O'Harris is not coming across as the sort of person who had enemies, quite the opposite. So that leaves me with one main suspect, and yet she does not appear to have a reason to kill her husband. Or at least none I can fathom. And I still haven't figured out the how, either."

"Was it Goddard O'Harris who had his body stolen?"

"Hidden, I think would be more precise, yes."

Annie nodded.

"Want me to ask around and see if anyone knows anything?"

"If you would, you never know, do you?"

"I'll keep my ears pricked," Annie grinned. "Now perhaps you should get off to bed before you fall asleep at that table."

Clara suddenly realised how heavy her eyes felt and how her body seemed to sag down. She shook herself awake.

"Yes, you are right. Oh, but I suppose we best get Tommy to bed first."

The ladies wandered to the parlour where Tommy Fitzgerald was still sound asleep in a chair.

"Almost seems a shame to wake him," Annie sighed.

"Think of the ache he will have in his neck tomorrow and the time he will spend moaning about it," Clara pointed out.

Annie stifled a laugh as Clara gave her brother a slight shake.

"Disturb a fellow..." muttered Tommy.

"Come on you," Clara grabbed one arm and hauled him up, while Annie swiftly moved in to grab the other.

"Can't a man sleep in peace?"

They escorted him awkwardly across the room. Tommy had lost the feeling in his legs during the war, or at least conscious feeling. When he was drowsy, or even half asleep as he was just then, his legs would move without thinking and it was possible to walk him towards his bedroom, as long as he was supported on both sides. Yet awake, no matter how hard he tried, Tommy could not manage to do the same.

The doctors labelled it as a mental barrier; some connection between his conscious thoughts and his legs was not being made. One had even suggested he was trying too hard. Now, as Clara helped him to his bedroom, she just wished he could see what he was achieving. As it was Tommy was on the cusp of sleep.

They rested him on his bed in the room that had once been the garden room.

"He sleeps like a baby," Annie smiled, taking off his shoes and socks.

"A troublesome baby," Clara snorted, pulling off his sweater rather brusquely, she had never been the best nurse.

"Let me, I know the routine," Annie said, taking the sweater and folding it neatly. "You need your sleep, you look exhausted."

"Do you mind?" Clara felt her shoulders sag just at the suggestion of weariness, she did feel like her hands and feet were full of lead.

"I was employed to be a nursemaid, remember?" Annie grinned. "A home help, I was supposed to be, I only took on the rest because we couldn't survive on the food you were cooking up."

Clara looked mildly offended, but she was too exhausted to really care.

"As long as you don't mind."

"Really, I don't."

Clara nodded and bid her maid goodnight, she left the room, pulling the door ajar in case Tommy cried out in the night. As she climbed the stairs, she heard Annie talking.

"Oh Tommy Fitzgerald, if only you could see yourself walking! If I could only make you see... I would do anything to prove to you these damn legs of yours can actually work!"

Chapter Nine

"Is Mrs Rhone in?" Clara asked the flustered looking reverend who answered the door with a cup of tea absent-mindedly cradled in his spare hand.

"Mother's Union, is it?" He asked.

"No. I believe we met the other night at Captain O'Harris' house?"

"Oh, is it raising funds for the unwed mothers again? I did rather think it was a poor show last time, Mrs Thwaite did cook those gorgeous crumpets and hardly any sold. I rather fear people have a thing against the unwed mothers' fund, I honestly can't think why."

Clara looked at the bemused man before her feeling a little confused herself.

"Perhaps people feel unwed mothers do not deserve help?" She offered.

"That is simply not possible, besides, it was for *charity*. Everyone knows one must give generously to the charity box. No, I fear it was hiring that lamentable singer that drove them away. Quite shocking she was, and after all those fine credentials she presented to me."

Clara endeavoured to keep a straight face as the reverend tailed off on a tangent.

"I should have known better, all that music hall business. She was really too racy for a church function. She used the word 'bloomers' you know."

"Really!" Clara tried to look as shocked as he had clearly been, she felt like patting the dear man on the shoulder and saying 'there, there.'

"Actually, I am not here about church business. I am here on behalf of Captain O'Harris and wondered if I could have a chat with Mrs Rhone?"

"Gladys is in the back parlour," the reverend Rhone ushered Clara into his vicarage. "I'm supposed to be writing a sermon, but I just can't seem to get the angle right. I fear I have become a little boring of late. Quite frankly, on occasions I have to catch myself from falling asleep during my own sermon."

"Oh dear," Clara said sympathetically.

"Are you a church goer?"

Clara hesitated.

"Before the war," she eventually admitted.

"Yes, that's just how it is. Quite depressing for myself of course, and no doubt God is rather miserable about it too. It was the war you know, never knew anything like it for thinning out my congregation."

Clara felt the vicar's choice of words slightly unfortunate.

"Of course, I expect things to pick up once people get over it. God is always there, after all. Actually, that might not be a bad catch for the sermon?" The vicar abruptly wandered off reciting his last words to himself.

Clara was left to find her own way about the vicarage and to the back parlour, which was a cramped room with the advantage of looking over the garden. Mrs Rhone was in the centre of it surrounded by piles upon piles of knitted squares, which she was busily sewing together. She looked up as Clara entered and removed her glasses.

"Miss Fitzgerald, isn't it?" She stood to greet her guest.

"Sorry to bother you Mrs Rhone when you are so busy."

"No matter dear, take a seat. These will take me days to sew together. There are several dear ladies who keep their ends of wool to knit assorted squares for blankets and then they pass them to me to sew up. I feel a tad put-upon every time they appear at my door with another bundle. But they are so intent on doing good. This latest batch is for the orphanage," Mrs Rhone, indicated the various piles that stood around her like stumpy pillars. "I don't suppose you sew…?"

Clara obligingly received a needle and a set of four squares to sew together.

"Now, pray tell me what brings you here?"

"Captain O'Harris' mystery brings me. He wants me to try and find the truth."

"That sounds like a good way to bring him more heartache. He believes his aunt guilty?"

"I think he would like me to prove otherwise," Clara perched two squares on her knee and began sewing with a long strand of green wool. "I thought I would pop by and have a little chat about the late Florence O'Harris. You knew her well, I presume?"

"Oh, my yes!" Mrs Rhone briefly looked up from her work to smile. "Florence Minerva Highgrove was my Sunday school teacher as a girl, before she married of course and became Florence O'Harris."

"Could you tell me a bit about her?"

"Well…" Mrs Rhone sucked at a strand of wool she was trying to thread into a needle, "she was pretty much like any girl. Let me see, she would have been eighteen when I was eleven, yes, that's about right, and she taught at the Sunday school until I was fifteen, and then she left to be wed. She would have been seventy-four this year, you know, that makes me feel rather old! Anyway, I always remember her as a young, quite forceful woman, who knew her own mind and would tell you as much. When she took our lessons, I always knew we were in for a good one, because she would read the bible stories with such flair and if you asked her a question, she would look you straight in the eye and ask a question right back. I know several of the older lads were besotted with her. My brother was fourteen and convinced he would take her to a dance one day, when he was old enough and had a penny or two. Of course, they were all downcast for a week when they heard she was getting married. Nothing lasts long at that age."

"How did she meet Goddard O'Harris?"

"I believe he was a connection of the family. Florence's father was in business and had done quite well for himself, her mother was a force to be reckoned with too. I always thought they must have come as quite a shock to dear Goddard, he was a bit too meek and mild for them! I'm not sure the exact way they met, but by the summer of 1866 they were walking out and a pretty pair they made. Goddard was quiet but handsome. He was studying at Cambridge as his father wished, but he rather fancied going into the army instead. I can picture them now, walking along the promenade, Florence looking pleased as punch with herself and Goddard trying to keep up with her."

"May I ask an indelicate question?" Clara interrupted, biting off her wool.

"What is it?"

"Did Florence marry for love, or..."

"Oh, I see what you mean. The O'Harris family was wealthy even then. I suppose they did rather eclipse the Highgrove fortune, but Florence was by no means poor," Mrs Rhone toyed with her needle. "I must admit, when I first heard I was a touch surprised. There was a rumour amongst us gals that Florence had secretly been writing to a young Royal Marine who had spent time at Brighton. Molly Durrant was adamant she had seen a letter Florence had written to a young man who was not Goddard, but Molly was a touch daft and not a good reader, so I never gave it any credit."

"But it might have been true?"

Mrs Rhone wrapped the thread from her needle round and round her fingers looking rather anxious.

"It's not the sort of thing I ever considered... but I do recall she used to mention a man called Edward, not often mind, but occasionally she would just slip and mention his name. I never thought it serious, but then again, I was eleven, and Florence was not from a poor family and her father was really quite liberal so I could see no reason as to why she could not have married a Royal Marine had she chosen to. No, she really must have married for love," Mrs Rhone spoke decisively and seemed to have settled the matter with herself.

"I suppose what I am trying to find out and, really, rather struggling with, is whether Florence had any reason to want her husband dead."

"That is an awful thought," Mrs Rhone shook her head glumly. "I really can't help you there because I did not know them well as a couple. Florence would come to church and help out at functions, but Goddard was rarely around. Then I met Isaiah, my husband, and I moved around for a time. We came back to Brighton in 1900 but it was only after Goddard's death that my acquaintance with Florence was refreshed. Let me tell you this Miss Fitzgerald, when I first encountered Florence O'Harris after all those years I hardly knew her. I said to myself, there is a woman whose heart has been broken. I never knew a creature look so sad and downcast. She never raised a smile in all those remaining years I knew her. I do not care what logic says or anything else, Florence loved her husband, and his passing pained her deeply."

Mrs Rhone went briefly back to her sewing. A clock in the front room ticked methodically and then chimed the hour. Clara slipped her needle through the woollen squares and let this new information sink in. If Florence had truly loved her husband, then his death was even more illogical.

Abruptly Mrs Rhone looked up.

"Have you found her diary?"

Clara ceased sewing too.

"No, I wasn't aware she wrote one."

"I am pretty certain she wrote one, right until her last days. I doubt it has been touched since her death. Her bedroom has not been altered, I believe. Captain O'Harris has enough rooms without interfering with his aunt's. Her diary should be there. I saw her carrying it once or twice. It was covered in green leather with a stamped detail of butterflies."

A ray of hope seemed to light up before Clara. This could provide vital new clues, of course she could hardly expect a confession written in the diary, but then again...

"Thank you, Mrs Rhone, I do apologise for disturbing you once again," Clara handed back her completed squares and Mrs Rhone took them with a curious look. "I must be on my way, goodbye."

Clara hurried from the room her mind whizzing with possibilities. No sooner had she gone Mrs Rhone gave a small sigh and started unpicking Clara's work.

Chapter Ten

Clara had developed a working relationship with the Brighton police after her last case when she had proved an asset to them for finding out information they could not. Inspector Park-Coombs had not initially approved of a woman poking her nose in his business, but his mind had been changed when he realised people would talk more openly to the friendly Clara Fitzgerald than his uniformed policemen. He had had to reluctantly confess she had proved herself rather a good detective. In recognition of her abilities, he had typed out a card with her name on it and his signature which would give her full access to police archives and (when suitable) police assistance at any time. Now Clara was going to use her 'free pass.'

When Inspector Park-Coombs had given Clara her token detective card she had almost turned it away. The events of that winter when she had become embroiled in her first murder case had taken their toll on her. She had come to wonder if her heart was really in solving mysteries, but time was a great healer and the distance of those dark days in January now made them feel much less grim. She wanted to solve this new mystery, she felt that renewal of excitement and enthusiasm that pulsed through her as she set her mind to work. The

O'Harris mystery was just what she needed to break her back into the detective business.

At the front desk of the Brighton police station, she flashed her card and asked if the inspector was about. The duty sergeant gave her a disapproving look then escorted her upstairs. The inspector was in his office supervising a two-man team of painters who were freshening up the station walls with a coating of whitewash.

"Miss Clara Fitzgerald," he cast her a knowing look as she approached. "I knew you wouldn't stay out of the detective business for long."

"Good morning, Inspector, having a little work done?"

"Oh, you know, had a little money left over in the budget and thought the old walls could do with sprucing up," the inspector cast a beady eye over the workmen. "Trouble is, I've nicked that one for stealing before now and I don't dare take my eye off him."

He pointed out the younger painter who seemed a little jittery under the gaze of the policeman.

"Have you a moment to talk?" Clara asked, ignoring the policing dilemma the inspector was facing.

"So, you have a new case?"

"Rather an old one that I am revising. Have you heard of the Goddard O'Harris mystery?"

The inspector broke into a broad grin.

"That old chestnut! Body vanishing in the night, no witnesses, no suspects, no murder weapon, quite a pickle. That was before I was inspector of course. You are looking into it then?"

"As best I can, time is not an asset when it comes to solving crimes I am realising. Were you on that particular case?"

"No, I was on day duty that week. Knew the fellows who were on it quite well though. They were a good lot, very professional. They told me the case was unsolvable and I believed them."

"Are there files on it?"

"Certainly, what little there was. Probably no more than a report but I can find it for you…" The inspector glanced at his workmen, torn between helping Clara and keeping his eye on the reformed criminal.

"Shall I watch them for you?" Clara offered.

"It is not a job for a woman," the inspector frowned.

"Neither is being a detective, perhaps we can avoid such sentiments?"

Inspector Park-Coombs let out a laugh then he swapped places with Clara and headed for the archives.

"If they cause you any trouble just call the sergeant!"

Clara watched him go and then sighed and sat down on the edge of his desk. She pulled a mirror from her bag and inspected her lipstick.

"Miss?" She looked up at the older painter who had visibly relaxed since the inspector's exit,

"Are you talking about that case where the old boy died and vanished from his own garden?"

Clara smiled at him.

"Yes I am."

"I've done some work at that hall, including on that airplane hangar in the grounds."

"Yes?"

"If he is still alive, and I can't say he is, but if he is, I should talk to the builder who hired us for the job. I remember him making a remark about the foundations a couple of days after the death."

"What sort of remarks?" Pressed Clara.

"Something about the concrete being all messed up, as if someone had been fiddling with it when it was drying, and one of the foundation trenches had been topped up with extra cement and it didn't match. We all wondered, you know."

The man finished abruptly and picked up his paintbrush to continue working. Clara considered what he had said, her thoughts had also gone to the barn when she first saw it. New constructions could prove a convenient place to hide things. She would have to find this builder.

"What was his name? The builder?"

"Mr Owen Clarence," responded the painter. "He used to live in Belgrave Street."

Clara nodded, taking a small diary from her handbag, and noting the name and address.

"Thank you."

"Do you reckon he was murdered, miss?" The painter had paused again.

"I think if he was not, someone went to a lot of trouble to hide an accident."

Inspector Park-Coombs appeared in the doorway with a thin cardboard folder which he handed to Clara.

"Peruse at your leisure," he said. "There is a friend of yours downstairs in the archives."

Clara looked up curiously.

"Oliver Bankes," the inspector looked mischievous. "He might have a picture or two that could be useful."

Clara had not given a thought to Oliver since she had last seen him on the pier fumbling with his camera and moaning about high-speed photography.

"You might like to take a look at some of the other files down there too. I noticed one other with the O'Harris name on it but wasn't sure it was related. You should take a look."

Clara knew when she was being politely route-marched into a meeting with Oliver Bankes.

"Thank you, Inspector," she said hopping from the desk. "I shall take a look."

"Do, and if you ever need to delve into the archives feel free," Park-Coombs had resumed his position in the doorway facing the painters. "Were these two any trouble while I was gone?"

"Quite the opposite," Clara smiled as she walked away and left the inspector to his supervising duties.

At first Clara was not sure she wanted to enter the archives and see Oliver. She was aware Mr Bankes was keen on her company and tried to involve himself in her cases as much as possible, but she wasn't sure about her own feelings on the matter, and she was uncomfortably aware of the time she had recently spent with Captain O'Harris. Why did she feel so guilty about such an innocent acquaintance? She was working for O'Harris, so naturally she would spend time with him, but she couldn't help a twinge of conscience as she toyed at the archives door before finally plucking up the courage to enter.

The archive was quite a small room, lined and divided by stacks of bookcases containing file after file of criminal activity. There was one window that had been blocked up and only allowed light to slip in through its top portion, and a measly bare bulb lit the remainder of the room. At the far side, a desk was positioned as close to the light sources as possible and stacked with forgotten folders and unfiled material. It was about what Clara had expected.

Bankes was at the desk going through some photos. He glanced up as she entered.

FLIGHT OF FANCY

"Hello Clara."

"Hello Oliver, what are you working on?"

Oliver lifted up a photograph of an artist's studio.

"There was a break-in at this place a few nights ago, stole some valuable pieces that had just been sold. I've been keeping my eyes open for the canvases, and I had a feeling I had seen one in a little gallery near the promenade."

"Would someone be so careless as to sell them like that?"

"Oh, you know how they think, give it a few days and the police will give up and besides a policeman can't tell a Picasso from a Rembrandt. Though to be honest I struggle a little with these paintings."

Clara glanced at the photo and noted several canvases decorated with random blobs of colour, horizontal lines, and multi-coloured splatters.

"This photo was taken for a lifestyle magazine a few weeks ago. Owners think this spurred the robbery."

"And you think?"

"That the owner is in debt and can claim compensation for the lost paintings as well as selling them a second time. I don't think they were genuinely stolen, you see."

"Well, Oliver, I didn't have you pegged as a detective."

"Didn't you?" Oliver grinned. "Art crime is a hobby; you would be surprised how much of it goes on."

"So, have you seen one of the canvases?

"Hard to tell, to be honest," Oliver shrugged. "Modern art and all that. What are you up to?"

"Exploring an ancient mystery, well, sort of. Ever heard of the O'Harris disappearance?"

Oliver paused and mulled over the question.

"Rings a bell, was it during the war."

"No, long before. 1913."

"I would have been 13," Oliver shrugged. "Must have slipped me by."

"Well, you aren't alone, it slipped me by too."

"How old were you in 1913 Clara?" Oliver asked slyly.

She glanced at him with a half-smile then carried on, ignoring the question.

"Goddard O'Harris dropped dead in his garden and then his body simply vanished. So far, I only have two witnesses, three if you count the gardener who saw the body."

"I always count gardeners," Oliver interjected solemnly.

"No clue to where the body went, how Goddard died or even what the motive might have been. I have only one suspect for moving the body, Mrs O'Harris."

"So where is the problem?"

"Too many unanswered questions. Why? How? Where? Captain O'Harris wants me to solve the mystery."

"Ah, Captain O'Harris."

Clara felt uncomfortable at the words, she almost blushed.

"He is quite the heartthrob among the ladies of Brighton, no doubt many would be jealous of you consorting with him."

Clara wasn't sure if Oliver was teasing her or probing for information.

"He is a paying client just like any other," she said stoutly.

"You haven't noticed he is handsome and dashing?"

"Have you?"

They stared at each other in uncomfortable silence, finally Oliver cleared his throat and put away his photographs.

"I best be on my way," he put the folder back on a shelf and started to walk to the door.

"No, please don't..." Clara bit at her lip, "I was a touch rude."

"I was only teasing you," Oliver said petulantly. "You quite snapped."

"I am a little tired of late," Clara excused herself brusquely. "And... I don't like my professionalism being called into question. I'm not helping O'Harris just because he is dashing and handsome."

"I know that," Oliver's grin returned. "So, you had noticed?"

This time Clara did blush.

"Oliver Bankes, sometimes you drive me to distraction!" Clara tutted. "He thinks his aunt killed his uncle and it is an awful thought to bear. He wants me to find out the truth, one way or another."

"And how do you intend to do that?" Oliver came back beside her.

"Like any puzzle, I suppose I shall just pick at it until I find a solution," Clara indicated the folder Inspector Park-Coombs had handed her. "He said there is another file with the O'Harris name on it, perhaps connected? This one looks rather flimsy."

She opened the folder and glanced at the rather uninspiring two slips of paper. One was a report from the duty sergeant about the call-out and the second was a record of the search the police had made the next day. There was nothing else.

"They didn't really try, did they?" Oliver said.

"I suppose there was so little to go on. What do you do if you haven't got a body or even know how a person died? Perhaps they thought it was a hoax and that Goddard had run off instead."

"With his mistress perhaps? And his wife claimed he had died and vanished to save face? That didn't happen, did it?"

"Colonel Brandt assures me Goddard O'Harris was quite dead, and I have no evidence of a mistress."

Oliver nodded.

"Shall we see about that other file?" He went to some shelves marked 1913 by a fading slip of paper and ran his fingers along the assembled folders. "Here it is. A touch thicker than the other file, but I wouldn't get your hopes up."

He brought the folder to the desk and opened it. They both looked at the top sheet.

"Goodness!" Remarked Clara. "Another murder!"

"It was ruled accidental," Oliver pointed out.

"A maid takes a tumble down the main staircase and your mind doesn't spring to foul play?" Clara flicked through the papers. "Ah, a post-mortem, and as I thought she was pregnant."

"I don't know whether to say you are just deeply clever or have a dreadfully suspicious mind," Oliver chuckled.

"I do not mind either. Accidental, my foot, the girl either threw herself down because of the shame or was pushed and whichever way you look at it that is murder to me."

"And a motive for Goddard's death?"

"I consider it very feasible. This happened 1912, a year later Goddard dies. That is time enough for someone to learn the truth and plan their revenge."

"It is always extraordinary fun having conversations with you," Oliver grinned. "I never know quite what to expect."

"I'm rather glad my morbid interests appeal to you," Clara replied. "Most people find them remarkably awful and prefer I don't discuss them."

"They are clearly very dull people then. Anything else I can do to help?"

"I wonder... do you suppose you may have some photos in your shop archives of the old O'Harris manor around that time?"

Oliver considered.

"Father may have taken some shots. Can't guarantee anything, but I will take a look."

"Thank you, Oliver," Clara smiled, suddenly very glad she had not turned away from the archive door.

"May I walk you home?" Oliver asked.

"Yes, you may," Clara responded.

Chapter Eleven

Captain O'Harris looked quite miserable when he opened the door to Clara the next day.

"Excuse my expression," he muttered as he ushered her inside. "I've received some bad news."

"I am sorry to hear that," Clara said, genuinely concerned to see this lively man so downcast. "Anything I can help with?"

"No, unless you can resurrect the dead. Sorry, that was poor taste," O'Harris slumped into a chair and waved a telegram at her. "Bertie Law, first-class pilot, and jolly good shot. Used to act as my gunner from time to time in the war and saved my backside more than once from the bloody Hun."

Clara realised the captain was a touch drunk.

"What happened to him?"

"Took a job on one of these Arctic explorations, aerial reconnaissance is all the rage. They build these little Arctic planes with enclosed cockpits and skis instead of wheels and pack 'em into boxes for the journey. Bertie went with a German party, the irony hah? He was to fly whenever he could and take photographs," O'Harris stared at the telegram. "His plane crash-landed into the ocean, took those bloody Huns two days to find him and it was too late. Poor chap died of hyperthermia."

O'Harris crumpled up the slip of paper and threw it on the floor.

"I'm sorry to hear that," Clara said gently.

"It's the shock of it that does you in. You know these planes are a bloody risky business, the *Buzzard* has had some near misses in her time, but you never really think it will happen. You tell yourself your luck will hold out for one more flight, one more dance across the sky."

"Then why do it?"

"Oh, for the thrill, for the buzz. To be in a plane and know you are one of the few to do just that and to stare down on a world so small below you and to be free of it for just a whisker of a second. If I couldn't fly, I think I would go mad, or perhaps go to sea. Bertie was the same, he had no intention of being land-locked once the war ended."

"Captain, is it Bertie's death that has so upset you or the thought that it could be you next?"

Captain O'Harris was stunned.

"He was my best friend and he plummeted into the Arctic Ocean and froze to death. I think that is a good enough reason to be upset."

Clara said nothing but looked thoughtfully at O'Harris, the silence stretched on until slowly a new expression crept onto the captain's face. This time it would be best described as morbid.

"I'm not a man who scares easy Clara."

"I thought as much," Clara nodded.

"I flew over those battlefields of France, looking down on mud and barbed wire and I never flinched. I don't mean to sound cocky because it is simply the truth. I never felt the fear of death like some men did, don't get me wrong those Huns shooting at you and the sudden arrival of one of their planes had my heart racing and my guts in knots, but I never thought for an instant that I would die. I was scared, but not enough to stop me flying and certainly not enough to think I was chancing my luck."

"And now?"

"Now life should be simpler. There aren't any enemy planes buzzing you, there aren't any guns firing for your wings or shells zipping through the air. If I felt almost safe then in my aircraft, surely I should feel all the more so now? Yet, instead... I don't know, I have this terrible dread rising in me."

"Dread?" Clara took a seat opposite him.

"It's like I don't believe in myself anymore, like I don't believe in the *Buzzard*. I keep thinking that if I try this record as I mean to, it will be my last flight," O'Harris stared bleakly ahead of him. "That telegram only made it clearer to me. In an instant you are gone. Bertie Law was a good pilot, but even a good pilot can't do anything if an engine fails, or the weather turns against you."

"But Bertie was flying in the Arctic," Clara tried to bring some rationality back to the captain's thoughts. "That has to be one of the most dangerous places to fly. You don't intend to be an Arctic aviator, do you?"

"No... I just keep thinking, what if it happens to me?" O'Harris shook his head sharply as if shaking out bad thoughts. "I'm glad your brother isn't here to see me like this Clara."

"He would understand."

"Maybe, but that's not the point," O'Harris took a long look at Clara. "I wasn't expecting you today, any news?"

"Nothing definite," Clara apologised. "But I wondered if I might look in your aunt's bedroom? I am told she kept a diary which might shed light on all this."

O'Harris gave a shrug.

"Never seen one but that doesn't mean it doesn't exist. You are quite welcome to look. I haven't set foot in her room since she died. Not that I ever went in it when she was alive! I imagine it is exactly as it was the day she passed."

"Then hopefully I shall find her diary. Are there any keys for the room? For locked drawers or a desk, perhaps?"

O'Harris pulled out his wad of house-keys.

"Think these are furniture keys," he showed Clara several small keys of various design. "I haven't found a purpose for them yet. Here, take the whole bundle."

Clara did as he said.

"Will you be all right while I take a look?"

"I have done the 'drowning my sorrows' part, now I just want to sit here and remember. Does it sound selfish to say I wish Bertie could have stayed on the ground, so I didn't have this shock to contend with mere days before *Buzzard's* flight across the Atlantic?"

"Perhaps a little selfish, but I understand it," Clara promised. "If he had made it, it would have filled you with confidence for your trip, instead it fills you with worry. But it mustn't, you are not Bertie Law, the *Buzzard* is not his plane, and you are not flying on an Arctic expedition."

"No," O'Harris nodded. "Too true. Look, will you stay for lunch? I'll have the cook rustle up a good spread. I don't feel like eating alone today."

"I'll stay," Clara said. "Now I best look at this room."

"Watch out for dust and woodworm," O'Harris managed a wan smile as she rose and headed out the room. "Top floor, third on the right, blue door."

The late Mrs O'Harris' room had the feel of a place out of time. Painted and decorated largely in shades of blue and cream, it had the atmosphere of a Victorian lady's boudoir, down to the four-poster bed with matching curtains and the old-fashioned washstand. Stepping inside was a bit like stepping into a drawing from an old book. The room had an atmosphere. Something slightly musty, but also eerily still, as though the room was holding its breath until the lady of the manor returned. Walking from the hall into the bedroom it felt as though Clara had entered another house, perhaps more curiously, it felt strangely lonely.

Clara absorbed the feel of the room. Perhaps she was foolish, but it crossed her mind that bedrooms could tell you a lot about a person, they were one of the most private rooms in a house, but also the most personal. This room kept the echoes of Mrs O'Harris, as though only a moment ago she had stepped across the threshold. It was a pause in time.

Clara moved about, feeling an intruder. A scent of lavender lingered in the air. Was this the room of a murderess or a grieving widow? Did Florence O'Harris lie on the bed and dream of her triumph or cry herself to sleep?

On the dressing table sat a brush and various half-empty cosmetics, several bottles of perfume were slowly turning to vinegar and a pretty vase sat bereft of fresh flowers. For a moment Clara thought of Florence coming to this very table and preparing her toilette for the day, looking in the mirror and seeing herself each day growing a fraction older. She opened the drawers of the table methodically, sorting through the debris of fifty years of life in the mansion. Old hair clips mingled with letters never replied to, clean handkerchiefs and old theatre programmes. Nothing revealing.

She moved on to a tall boy and worked through the drawers. Again, there was nothing but clothes, mainly undergarments and stockings.

Each drawer gave a new waft of the lavender fragrance as it was opened, for a moment bringing the elusive Florence a touch closer.

The bedside table was more promising because the top drawer was actually locked. Kneeling, Clara went through the bundle of keys O'Harris had handed her selecting the smallest ones from the ring and trying them each in turn. None seemed to work. She tried them all and then sighed to herself. A little disappointed she decided to try again just in case and worked through the keys until she reached one that was rather short and stocky and didn't look the least promising. Clara pushed it into the lock and rattled it around, for a moment it jammed then, suddenly, she felt it turn. The drawer clicked open, and Clara could only hope her effort was about to be rewarded.

In the drawer were further letters, but these ones were more personal than the general correspondence in the dressing table. There were several letters from Florence's sister-in-law, Captain O'Harris' mother. A few others were from Goddard and appeared to be love letters, even if they were a bit dry and rambling. Goddard was clearly not a poet. Clara placed them all on the bed intending to go through them for clues when she had time.

The drawer contained a lot of knickknacks partially hidden under a lace shawl that had been wedged inside. A silver pincushion in the shape of a pig jostled for space with a bone letter-opener and several miniature glass bottles semi-full of all manner of old liquids. It was rather disappointing. Clara fumbled in the drawer and found a few lost assorted buttons and a hatpin that pricked her finger. Cross at her own carelessness and feeling foolish for not thinking of it before she went to remove the shawl so she could examine the drawer properly. It was then she realised the shawl was a lot heavier than it should be. Unfolding it, she had to smile as she revealed three leather-bound books, the top one being green with butterflies tooled into the cover.

"I found your diary Florence," Clara whispered to herself.

Strangely, she did not feel the need to rush downstairs and show her prize immediately to O'Harris. Instead, she sat on the bed which groaned in the manner old beds do and thumbed through the first and newest of the diaries. Though not all the entries were dated, it seemed to chart Florence's life from the year 1900 onwards, there were great gaps, sometimes as much as a month, before feverish, dedicated entries charting life in Brighton almost by the hour. She turned the pages to 1913 and looked for the entries closest to the time of Goddard's death.

There was no entry on the day of his actual demise, that would have been too fortunate, reflected Clara, but there was one piece vaguely dated Oct. '13, which was apparently written at the time of his funeral.

Oct. '13

Despondent. No time like present for new charity drive but have not the energy. Mrs B. keeps asking when we can discuss the flower festival. Can't think about that. So lonely here. Have asked young John to visit, perhaps a little youthfulness will chase away the gloom. Feel like Goddard is everywhere, yet nowhere. Turn a corner and expect to see him.

Just collected apples from orchard. Poor harvest, wasps too numerous. Should have done it earlier. Can't seem to get on top of things. Cook wants to make apple pie, but I shan't eat it. Was Goddard's favourite, would feel disrespectful. Have dreadful headache. Should sleep but another visit due from Mrs M. about Church social. Really hate all this. Wish they would leave me alone.

Clara paused in her reading. Florence might have seemed a tough, even hard character on the outside, but clearly inside she felt things as strongly as any person. She also seemed to have grieved deeply for the loss of her husband.

"Could you really have killed him?" Clara said to herself as she read on.

Mr C. wants to know about the 'barn.' I suppose it should be finished as Goddard wanted. Only the foundations have been dug and it would not take a moment to grass it back over, but I cannot bring myself to do that. I shall not sell Goddard's cars and they must have a home. Maybe when it is finished, I shall feel some peace.

Letter from John arrived. He is coming soon. Haven't seen him since the funeral and now I regret inviting him. What can I say to him when I see him? I feel such guilt over Goddard. I wish I could make it right.

"Miss?"

Clara snapped the diary shut as a maid appeared at the door.

"Sorry to bother you miss but luncheon will be ready in about half an hour, the captain wanted to let you know."

"Thank you," Clara smiled at her, and the maid vanished again.

She sat for a moment; the appearance of the maid had reminded her of the other incident that had marred the O'Harris' home-life. She returned to the diary and flicked back several pages until she arrived at 1912. The maid had fallen to her death in the spring of that year, Clara turned to the entries in the diary just before.

Chapter Twelve

April '12

John has been paying a visit all week, I am quite exasperated by his presence. He seems to be everywhere I go, but Goddard is pleased to see him. He has been gloomy of late after his spell of influenza, and it does him good to have a young person about. He has come up with this idea of a huge 'barn' to house his cars. He tells me it is a thing called a garage which is all the rage in America. I am disinclined towards the idea.

John went home today. Goddard sullen again.

Millie, the new girl, has not come downstairs to sweep the hearths. Cook has apologised and says the girl has eaten something that disagreed with her. It was her afternoon off yesterday and she went into town, perhaps she ate something there. I hope this does not become habit.

Millie appeared today. Looks rather pale. Told her if she's infectious she could stay away, but she said she just had a bad oyster while she was in Brighton. It shall not hurt her; the girl is growing rather fat and if *she carries on will need a new uniform. It will have to come out of her pay, I am generous enough as it is.*

Terrible accident today. Millie tumbled down the stairs. Goddard says maybe the food poisoning made her giddy. Doctor has pronounced her dead and police had to come. Feel bad about my last comments. Poor lass left behind a mother and three younger sisters.

May '12
Inquest on Millie today. Cannot bear to go, feel something was deeply wrong.

Verdict came back as accidental, but coroner revealed Millie was with child. Goddard told me. Don't know who the father was, cook doesn't think she had a sweetheart. Seemed such a quiet girl. Having terrible thoughts. John was here at Christmas, and I remember seeing her talking to him and laughing. Told Goddard I want to go away for a while, but his gout is bad again. Instead have to face the Mothers' Association with this hanging over me.

Roses have started to bud, have cut a few to put in water and wait for them to bloom. Wisteria is looking vibrant this year. Thinking of planting some new strawberry bushes in the kitchen garden, cook has an inkling for gooseberries...

Clara scanned the next few entries, but Aunt Florence had seemed to suddenly find more interest in her gardening than the fate of Millie. There was something unsettling about the sudden change of subject, it almost felt as though Florence was shoving the matter to the back of her mind for better or worse. Or was she reading too much into this?

After all a great deal of time may have elapsed between the first May entry and the last, perhaps Millie's accident had drifted from peoples' minds. But what were these terrible thoughts Florence was having? And had she been suggesting what Clara thought she had?

Gathering her 'treasure' Clara made her way downstairs and went to find O'Harris. He was in the dining room looking less miserable and more his usual self. There was a glass of water by his hand and a clutch of aspirin pills.

"Trying to stem the tide," he shrugged apologetically to Clara. "Did you find anything?"

"Odds and ends," Clara sat the diaries on the table, but did not offer them to the captain. "Your aunt was not terribly open even in her diary."

"She was rather a closed book, excuse the pun."

"It seems that way, still, would you mind if I took these to read? Might give me an idea or two?"

"Of course, if it helps."

"I'll bring them back when I am done."

"So, what does Auntie Flo write about?"

"Gardening a lot of the time," Clara looked away and tried to appear nonchalant. "There was one little thing that caught my eye. A story about a girl Millie? I believe she was a maid here?"

O'Harris went a touch pale, at least Clara thought he did.

"Millie had an accident," he said rather dully.

"Yes, I did have this notion it could be connected to your uncle's death. Perhaps he knew something he should not?"

"Millie threw herself down the stairs because she found she was pregnant," O'Harris said.

"Threw? Or was she pushed?" Clara met his eyes, they looked at each other for a moment.

"You have no need to play games with me Clara," O'Harris said sadly. "You are too sharp to fool me into thinking you could be this dull."

"Was Millie murdered?" Clara said, cutting to the chase.

"I wasn't here when it happened, so I cannot say," O'Harris sighed. "I always thought it was suicide."

"Who was the father of her child?"

"You've guessed that too."

Clara shook her head.

"No, rather it was your aunt who guessed, or should I say suspected. She had seen you together at Christmas laughing, I suppose it looked a little cosy for comfort."

"Then I suppose there is no point beating about the bush, Millie and I... we had a bit of a fling that Christmas. It was nothing serious, at least I didn't think so. Millie was quite a confident thing. Would you believe me if I said I felt more liked the seduced then the seducer?"

"I imagine you would know."

"That is harsh, Clara. Do you think that badly of me?" He stared at her, and Clara felt a touch bad.

"You are a charmer captain. You are dashing and lively and good fun to talk to. I can only say that, from an outside perspective, I find it hard to imagine you have any difficulty attracting women."

"And I don't, not now. But in my younger days I didn't have this confidence. The war gave me my wings Clara, in more ways than one. But back in 1912 girls still had the power to scare me, especially attractive girls. I won't deny I encouraged Millie, but she was not bashful or meek. To be blunt, I don't think I was her first lover."

Clara didn't know what to say to such talk. On the one hand her sympathies went out to Millie, and she found herself thinking of her as the wronged innocent. The seduced girl who found herself pregnant and killed herself in despair. But on the other hand, she had no reason to assume O'Harris could be callous or cruel, nor that he was lying. Yet it was hard to tie together the image of wronged Millie, with the image of her as an experienced woman of the world.

"I suppose whichever way you look at it I shall come out wrong," O'Harris sagged in his chair. "I didn't know she was pregnant until after, if that is any comfort."

"She didn't tell you?"

"No. I must admit that puzzled me, I thought she would have done. I would have taken care of her, you know."

"I do believe that Captain."

"At least that is something," O'Harris took a gulp of water and swallowed another aspirin. "What more can I tell you? I always thought it was an accident."

"It may have been, but it is just a rather startling coincidence."

"Can you find out for certain?"

Clara took a moment to think.

"Perhaps if I were to know who was in the house at the time, and where, I could make a guess. There is another possibility, however."

"What is that?"

"Millie *did* take her own life, but someone thought she did not, or they blamed someone for her suicide, for getting her pregnant. And how far would you look but to the lord of the manor?"

O'Harris suddenly perked up.

"Are you suggesting this may offer up more suspects? That Auntie Flo could be off the hook?"

"I wouldn't get carried away just yet, but I think it is something to bear in mind. Could you provide me with a list of servants in the house in 1912?"

"Certainly!"

O'Harris jumped to his feet and began rooting for a pencil and paper in a nearby bureau when a serving girl appeared with two platters of food.

"Put them on the table," O'Harris motioned without looking.

The girl smiled at Clara and placed down the two platters, removing their lids without looking.

"Chicken liver pâté and smoked salmon sandwiches… oh my Lord!" The lid of the platter fell to the floor with a crash.

O'Harris turned sharply and looked from the stunned maid who had her hands to her mouth, to Clara who was calmly picking a dead mouse out of the decoratively arranged dish of pâté.

"Good Heavens! What has been going on in the kitchen?" O'Harris said appalled.

"I should say a great deal," Clara indicated a small label around the mouse's neck. Printed in block capitals upon it, in black ink, were the words 'LEAVE THE PAST ALONE.'

"It's a warning," the colour drained from O'Harris' face.

"I know," said Clara. "It's my first, I confess to being a touch excited."

O'Harris gave her a curious look.

"Excited?"

"Well, it means I am on the right path," Clara explained eagerly. "It wasn't Aunt Flo who committed the crime, it was someone else, someone who is still alive and doesn't want any trouble."

"But only cook and the housekeeper have been here that long."

"Could be either of them, or then again it could be someone from outside the house who snuck in while food was being prepared. By the way, your gardener has been here that long too."

"Has he?"

Clara shook her head at the captain.

"You must pay attention, now this is really very good news. I was starting to think I was going off on a tangent and letting my imagination run away with itself. This proves my instincts were right," Clara handed the mouse to the servant girl, who took it with a look of revulsion by the tail. "Please dispose of that and bring a fresh tray of pâté."

The girl left holding the mouse as far from her as possible.

"You know she will report all this to anyone she speaks to," O'Harris looked worried.

"Yes, I know. It is quite delightful. I finally feel like a real detective, and you know the best news of all?"

"No, do tell?"

"This means that in all probability the murderer is still alive!" Clara's eyes sparkled. "It means I could actually bring your uncle's killer to justice!"

Chapter Thirteen

D^{ec '12}
Goddard rather peaky since his brother's death. Tragic to lose a younger brother. He won't eat. Keeps fretting. I imagine I shall miss poor Oscar too, shame about the cancer, nasty business.

Reading of the will, usual stuff. Oscar knew he was dying and left a few special gifts to his family. He bequeathed me a pretty Victorian vase of his mother's that I had always admired, and to Goddard a box of expensive cigars. Goddard hasn't the heart to smoke them. Rest of Oscar's money went to John, poor lad has no one except us since Susan's death.

"Captain O'Harris' mother was called Susan?" Tommy looked up from the diary he was reading.

"Yes, she was an actress I think, haven't got to that part yet," Clara was going through the letters she had gathered from the hall.

"I get the impression Aunt Florence didn't get on with her."

"My impression is that Florence did not get on with anyone, or at least it sounds like it from her diary."

"Waspish is, I think, an appropriate word for her manner."

Clara laughed.

"Exactly, I have been trying to think of the right term all day!"

Tommy made a note on a piece of paper beside him and then closed the diary and faced his sister.

"I am beginning to have a feel for what Florence was like, but Goddard is another matter. I can't get a handle on him."

"He just seems to have been nice."

"Nice? What sort of thing to be is that? That's the sort of thing you say about someone when you don't know what else to say and when you would rather avoid speaking the truth. No one is ever completely 'nice'."

"You're a cynic, Tommy."

"There was a lad in the trenches, joined us in '17. Small, quiet, frightened of his own shadow and a bit of a loner. He always seemed to be around when you wanted to change your trousers, not that we did that often, but if you did you could guarantee he was suddenly there and watching. No one really wanted to be chummy with him, polite, yes, but not pally. When he bought it in early '18 the chaplain asked us for a few words about him he could send back to his parents. All we could think of was 'he was nice'."

"I get your point. And I agree Goddard is rather a mystery, but I am running out of people to interview on the subject and the diaries have proved another dead-end so far."

"Anything in the letters?"

Clara gave a sigh and sorted through the papers beside her.

"Nothing much, usual thing, letters to friends and to her mother. Really can't see why she kept them so close in her bedside table, they are rather every day, except for one which congratulated her on her wedding."

"That's the trouble with letters, you only get to see one side. We'll never know what Florence wrote in hers."

"Judging by the diaries, not a lot," Clara leaned back in her chair and stretched her neck. "Go on then, tell me I am looking for things that aren't there."

"The mouse could have been a practical joke," Tommy shrugged, he had at first been angry to know his sister had been presented with a dead rodent and a warning, but slowly this had waned to a feeling that it was all a little too dramatic. Real murderers did not go around leaving notes on dead mice, it was the sort of thing you found in books.

"I think I am on to something," Clara replied. "I've still got that builder to talk to. The body had to go somewhere."

"All right, say you dig up the barn and find Goddard O'Harris, it still could make his death accidental."

"But unlikely."

"And you have yet to even hypothesise a murder weapon."

"That is my biggest hurdle," Clara admitted. "If we rule out an external weapon, a knife or bullet say, by the lack of any wounds – which we have to accept at face value from the witnesses – then we come to a rather short list of alternatives. Ruling out natural conditions such as a bad heart, we have to look at either a long-term poison that just happened to act at that moment in the garden or something hazardous Goddard inhaled, a gas or something."

"Have you looked for a poison that takes a long time to act?"

"Was hoping you would," Clara smiled.

"Thought as much. I'll have Annie worried again when she goes to pick up my library books. Right, and the gas is a non-starter because where would it come from?"

"Exactly. I recall stories of things like pockets of thin air in caves that can kill a man quickly, but not in an English garden."

"What about something he was injected with before he died?" Tommy thought out loud. "An over-dose of something, say morphine?"

"He wasn't taking any such medicine as far as I am aware, though Mrs Rhone did mention a wasting disease. I suppose you are suggesting an accident again?"

"I was also thinking, what if it was suicide and Florence wanted to hide the fact of what her husband had done? It would be easy enough to get the good Colonel on board and then she hid the body to prevent anyone learning the truth."

"Why?"

"Because of the shame? Or because she thought it might rekindle suspicions about his role with that maid? You know, he topped himself over remorse at getting her pregnant and then her dying?"

"All theories and nothing definite."

Tommy shrugged again.

"Right now, I am finding the Goddard mystery a little hopeless. Unless you can find a motive, other than this notion of a connection with the dead maid, then we really seem to be up a creek without a paddle."

"Oh, don't say that," Clara pulled the diaries towards her. "There must be something, here you look at the letters."

Tommy casually glanced through the papers.

"What of that fellow who was supposed to be involved with her?"

Clara returned her brother's shrug.

"Rather vague, Mrs Rhone thought it was a load of nonsense made up by another girl. He was in the army, I think."

"What division?"

Clara groaned.

"Honestly Tommy, he is a very random loose end, I didn't even get his name. He probably didn't exist."

"Was he a Royal Marine?"

Clara hesitated.

"He might have been, why?"

"The wedding congratulations letter, it is from Edward Highgrove, RM. That stands for Royal Marine."

Clara took back the letter.

"I assumed he was a cousin, because he had the same surname as Florence."

"Perhaps he was."

"And also, he referred to his own wife in the letter..." Clara stared at her brother. "If Edward Highgrove was the other man, the man she loved..."

"And he was married, so she could not have him."

"Then she married Goddard as second-best, maybe even to spite Edward."

"And that letter to me sounds like a farewell note. He cut her adrift, look here he says, 'I think you have made a wise choice, let me wish you fondest congratulations from myself and Mrs Helen Highgrove.' He could not have made it plainer that he had a wife, he could have just said 'Helen,' but he spelt her name out in full. He was cutting ties."

"She kept it all these years, a letter so full of heartache. She never forgot him."

"And she never forgot she married Goddard because her true love abandoned her."

"But Tommy, we have just given Florence a better motive for killing her husband."

They looked at each other forlornly. At that moment Annie appeared.

"Begging pardon, but a Colonel Brandt is on the telephone. He wants to speak to Clara." Annie looked puzzled, clearly, she had thought a colonel would only want to speak to Tommy.

"Ah, one of my star witnesses," Clara moved from her chair. "Probably wanting to know how I am getting on."

"Ask him about Edward!" Tommy hissed as his sister left the room.

Colonel Brandt sounded breathless on the phone, he 'ummed' and 'ahhed' a lot as he exchanged pleasantries with Clara. He seemed uncomfortable.

"Colonel Brandt, you sound rather put-out?" Clara went straight to the heart of the matter.

"Well, I've wrestled this phone off the butler at the club. He says I am only allowed ten minutes."

"Then perhaps we better skip to the reason you rang?"

"Ah, yes," Brandt went quiet for a moment. "Are you making any progress?"

"Not a great deal," Clara admitted. "Other than an interesting coincidence of a maid dying at the hall."

"Oh that? 1912, wasn't it? Nothing to do with Goddard."

"I have established that, only someone else might think differently."

"Like whom?"

"That I have yet to determine. Did you have something to tell me Colonel?"

"Just was thinking, that's all," the colonel fell into silence briefly again. "The other night when we discussed Goddard, well, it occurred to me I had not been entirely honest with you. Goddard was a good man and a good friend, but no one is perfect, and I fear I may have been too conscientious in presenting my old friend's reputation as spotless. Truth is Goddard had his secrets like all of us."

"Anything in particular?" Clara asked.

"I have to say I have given that a lot of thought. I mean, there were odd things, awkward words between Goddard and the old captain of the golf club, an argument with the council about replacing the old hospital with more housing, that sort of thing, but people don't kill over such mundane matters."

"Not usually."

"Then it came to me, there was one thing that was very pertinent and could present a motive for Goddard's killer."

Clara perked up. Just what she was looking for!

"What is it Colonel?"

"The thing is, I would rather not talk on the telephone. Could you come down here?"

Clara glanced at the clock, it was a little before two and it would not take her more than a few moments to walk to Brandt's club.

"I can be there in half an hour."

"That would be grand. I shall wait for you in the lobby."

Clara put the phone down, a ripple of excitement racing through her. Just as she thought the case had gone cold it had come alive again. She went back into the parlour and explained where she was going.

"Will you be back for dinner?" Annie asked.

"Probably," Clara grinned, feeling excited at this new lead, and rushing to grab up her hat and gloves.

Chapter Fourteen

She arrived at the club completely distracted and found the colonel waiting in the lobby as he had promised. He hurried her through into the guest parlour before the butler had a chance to cast a sneer at them.

"I am very grateful you came so soon. Can I offer you afternoon tea?"

Clara waved away the suggestion.

"I cannot this afternoon Colonel, thank you for the offer."

"I'm sorry to disturb you when you must be busy. Life as a female detective must be hectic."

"It can be, but there are just as often quiet patches when you can't wish hard enough for someone to drop in or write a letter," Clara took a seat. "You sounded quite anxious on the telephone Colonel, if you don't mind my saying."

"I am feeling a touch..." the colonel shook his head. "Honestly, I don't know what I am feeling, all I know is that I had to talk to you and be honest. Goddard was my friend, and I won't help find his killer by hiding my head in the sand and making out he was the perfect man. He was not Miss Fitzgerald, none of us are."

"On that I shall concur," Clara smiled. "I think we would be all rather boring if we were perfect."

"Everyone keeps describing Goddard as 'nice.' Do you know how much I hate that word? Nice is meaningless. In my day if you had a soldier die in your unit and you couldn't think what to say about him you wrote 'he was nice.'"

Clara nodded, reminded of Tommy's sentiments.

"To be honest, I'm rather sick of pretending there was nothing but harmony between Goddard and Florence, I feel as though I am in some awful play and describing off-scene characters the audience never get to meet. They were flesh and blood people, friends, yet I feel like I'm discussing strangers when I open my mouth. It's my own fault, I just don't want to speak ill of the dead."

"You cannot speak ill when you are only telling the truth," Clara pointed out. "Besides, Goddard's killer may still be alive and that means they can still be caught."

The colonel nodded unhappily.

"I've been thinking about that too. It makes me unbearably miserable to think Flo might have done him in."

The colonel looked deeply glum.

"The more I think about it the more it crosses my mind that she could have done it," he continued. "Under the right circumstances with the right push... I feel awful just saying it."

"No one has condemned her yet and, if it is any consolation, I have come across some documents that imply that Florence had a genuine affection for her husband, even if it was deep down."

"Yes, Flo could seem hard I admit. She would give her life for you though. I once had a bit of a scrape with some lads down by the pier.

Silly stuff, all of us trying to throw our weight around and me fresh in uniform. I took the worst of it. Flo came to visit me in the hospital. I'll never forget that. She came in, called me a silly fool, and brought me the evening papers. It was her way, you know."

"Colonel," Clara smiled, "you don't make her sound like a cold-blooded murderess."

"Well, you better just hear the rest of what I have to say before you hold to that conclusion," the colonel groaned as he sat in a chair. "Damn lonely business getting old. Mark my words girl, if you get the opportunity get married so you have someone to complain to when you are old and grey, and the world seems to have left you behind."

"Do you feel left behind, Colonel?"

The colonel shook his head sadly.

"I don't know, just seems the world has changed so much... I really do miss Flo and Goddard. They were like rocks in a heavy sea. You could cling to them even while everything about you was in turmoil and change. These last thirty years have shook us all and nothing seems the same as when I was a lad. Not that I think we can stay the same or that all change is bad, but it is a touch frightening, that's all. And that last war..." the colonel shuddered. "I hope I never have to go through a thing like that again."

"As do we all," Clara concurred whole-heartedly. "But what was it you called me here for?"

The colonel moved in his seat uncomfortably, pulled a cushion away and then replaced it with another. After an endless amount of faffing about, he seemed to settle and prepare himself to speak.

"Goddard was a good friend, but he was older than me and you can't expect a man of his age to confide his secrets in a lad, even once I was in uniform and pushing through the ranks. Goddard was secretive, I think that is the way to describe it. He certainly had done things he would not talk about, and you had the impression that he thought things he would never dare speak. He was not wicked or mean, or any of those other things that are associated with secretive people, but he was extremely quiet, and you had the feeling that was not natural for him. As if he was pointedly quiet because he feared what might happen if he did open his mouth.

"I told you he talked about the Boer war to me? Always the same stories, a handful of accounts, but I knew there was more, so much more, he just never chose to tell me them. That is what I mean about him being secretive and quiet. He kept himself locked away. I think deep down he was a man who hurt a lot, who ached inside and couldn't feel the love others around him tried to show him. I've seen a lot of young men like that since the war, it is what has made me reflect on my old friend. I see him in a new light. I think he was scarred."

The colonel jostled the cushions again, it seemed to help him to overcome his reticence.

"Goddard was not easy to love. I said I would be honest and there it is. Flo was remarkable to stick with him. He wasn't aggressive, or cruel. I never knew a man less inclined to violence of any description, I think that was an after-effect of the Boer conflict, but if he had few negatives, he also had few positives. You couldn't talk about deep matters with Goddard, he never spoke of his feelings. If you asked him what something meant to him, it was generally greeted with a shrug and silence, no matter if you were discussing a painting or the death of a loved one. Some days I just wanted to stare into his eyes and catch a glimpse of the soul within, otherwise I at times felt I was talking to nothing more than an automaton programmed with facts and figures about historic battles.

"I never saw him kiss his wife. Nor touch her. I know some men are like that, never an inch of emotion shown in company, but I doubt he was different when they were alone. I don't suppose Flo's demeanour helped. It's why they never had children, you know, they both could have, but they never..." the colonel faltered. "Goddard admitted it to me once when we had both drunk a little too much. One of the rare times he stepped out of his self-imposed silence. He regretted it of course and was even more conservative in his speech the next time we met. I thought nothing would ever change that, then Susan O'Harris waltzed into our lives."

"Susan O'Harris? Captain O'Harris' mother?"

"Yes, Susan. Married Oscar O'Harris around 1880. He was a good deal younger than Goddard and as different from his brother as can be. Oscar was a laugh, but he was also impetuous and quick to anger. I found him a little too forceful after the reserve of Goddard, not that I knew him until after the heat had died down from his marriage to Susan."

"Yes, it was somewhat of a scandal, I believe?"

"Susan was an actress, now that can mean a lot of things, but I am confident in her case it was a genuine career with no side-lighting in other occupations, if you understand what I mean?"

"I do." Clara nodded; she was well aware that many a woman of ill-repute termed herself an actress to side-step notoriety.

"She was in the music halls. Singer. Dancer. Nothing special, all the bit parts, but she earned a living and that was what mattered. Susan loved performing, she would sing her heart out if you asked and she *could* sing. I always thought it a shame she was so ignored, some of these fine lady singers we have today do not have a thing on Susan, but I suppose I am biased. We were all a little in love with her, you see.

"I think it was 1883 or 1884 she appeared with Oscar at the old house. It had been arranged, nothing out of the blue about it like some say. Admittedly Oscar was down on his luck and hoping to negotiate an allowance off his older brother. Susan was vivacious, she sparkled. She entered the house like a ray of light. It was before the time of movies, but she could have been one of those stars on the screen. She just radiated life and energy. She was around my age, don't forget, and I fell in love the instant I saw her. I wanted to whisk her off that instant. I made all sorts of ridiculous plans in my mind for taking her with me to India where I was due to be based soon. I could picture her in a native sari, lounging about my grand house in the heat of the Indian sun. Of course, I never had the guts to speak to her.

"Next to her we all felt a little... drab. Even Flo seemed affected. Susan was a vision, but Oscar, well, he looked a little worn about the edges. Poverty doesn't come easy to a man used to money. From what I gathered they had been living off Susan's earnings the last three years and it had been a struggle.

"Their visit was not an easy one. Oscar and Goddard argued, it was all about money. Oscar wanted his fair-share of the inheritance their father had left, but Goddard was reluctant to just hand it over. I think he doubted his brother would look after it wisely. He preferred the idea of giving him a set amount each year, but that made Oscar feel tied to him. Every day they retired to the office after lunch and every day they argued. I had never heard Goddard raise his voice before then."

The colonel shifted uncomfortably in his seat. Clearly speaking like this of his friend was far from easy.

"Had it always been a fiery relationship?" Clara asked gently.

"I cannot tell you," the colonel shook his head. "Perhaps it was because Goddard was older."

"Perhaps."

"Anyway, these arguments went on and on. I was around quite a lot just then on leave and I could hear the whole calamity. Flo looked utterly morbid about it, clammed right up and barely uttered a word.

The only person I had to talk to was Susan," the colonel gave a sad smile. "Now she *was* a talker. Her words could soothe a lion, they dripped like champagne from her tongue. I honestly thought I was in love with her, I thought she was the only woman I could ever love after that, and, of course, in the end, it was her who secured Oscar's money."

The colonel glanced aimlessly at the clock in the room, letting the time tick by as the memory of those long-ago days played before his eyes.

"Is this the matter you wished to discuss? Money troubles with Oscar?" Clara gave him a mental nudge when a minute had ticked by.

"No," the colonel took his eyes off the clock reluctantly. "No, it was more serious than that."

Clara settled back for further revelations.

"You see, at the time I never could quite fathom how Susan did it, how she persuaded old Goddard to climb off his high horse and virtually roll over backwards for his brother. I think Flo was baffled too, but we both supposed she had laid on the charm pretty thick and Goddard had felt sorry for her. It didn't even occur to me..." the colonel closed his eyes and grimaced. "I've lain awake thinking about what I must tell you, it goes against the grain. I was loyal to Goddard, always loyal, and I swore to guard his secrets to my very grave."

"Did he have many secrets that needed guarding?"

"Maybe. But I only ever knew a handful, and I never saw a problem in exerting my duty over them until now," the colonel rubbed at his chest. "All this nonsense has given me the most dreadful indigestion."

"I am sorry to put you through this Colonel, but I think you would feel better if you told me. Obviously, it must be important."

"That damn Susan," Brandt shook his head again. "She was a harpy and we never realised it. She stood in our midst looking like an angel when deep down she was a devil playing her own game. I've thought some things about her since that first meeting and since I saw through her disguise. Did she marry Oscar expecting money? Oh, I think she did, and was it her who persuaded him to go see his brother? Yes, I think that is true too. And she presented herself to us as nothing more than a harmless innocent, but I see now she was really an evil creature at heart."

"What did she do Colonel?" Clara wondered what could have changed the colonel's mind so firmly.

"She seduced Goddard!" The colonel suddenly snapped, surprising them both. "I know, I know we talk of restraint, but she was different. Anyone she threw herself at faltered. You know the charm young O'Harris has? Well imagine that in female form along with a soul completely devoid of moral fibre. That is how she got her money. She seduced Goddard and held the shame over his head until he promised to give Oscar his money. She would have told Flo otherwise, Goddard explained that to me himself. He was so guilty about it all, he had never been unfaithful to Flo despite their awkwardness. Then there was the matter of his inability to..."

The colonel stood up and began to pace.

"A man's private life should be private!" He stormily said to no one in particular.

"May I interpret what you were going to say for you?" Clara offered.

Colonel Brandt looked at her apologetically.

"He could not make love to his wife," he said before Clara could offer her opinion. "I have to say it for you to understand. He could not make love to his wife, but he could make love to that harlot. Do you see the shame and guilt that made him feel? And if poor Flo ever knew it would destroy her. I don't think any man could feel so sickened by his infidelities as Goddard."

"Yet, there is no motive for a crime if no one, aside from yourself, knew of this matter." Clara pointed out delicately.

"Oh Miss Fitzgerald, if only that were so. But the harpy told her husband. Not immediately mind, no, this was on her death bed. A guilty soul confessing before she met with her maker."

"When did Susan O'Harris die?"

"1900. John was eight," the colonel slumped back down on the sofa. "She had no other children, you know. Oscar was sterile, so the doctors said. He called John a miracle and mocked the medical men who had told him he could never be a father. That harpy couldn't even allow the poor man that consolation. She told him that his son was in fact his nephew and that Goddard O'Harris was John's father."

Clara let the revelation sink in. It explained a thing or two, including Goddard's increasing interest in his nephew's life and achievements. Perhaps it even explained the kindness shown by Florence O'Harris, the woman who appeared cold but in fact could care extraordinarily deeply about others.

"Does Captain O'Harris know?"

Brandt shook his head.

"Goddard told me after he received a letter from Susan telling him what she had done. It was the last thing she ever wrote. Whether he told Florence I don't know, but no one ever told John. I have no idea if Goddard ever spoke to his brother Oscar after that."

"But Oscar was dead by 1913, so he could not take revenge, if that is what you are implying. You realise you have cast Florence even more into the role of potential murderess?"

"I know, I know," Brandt clutched his head in his hands. "But I knew I had to tell you. I had to give you the facts else you could never solve this matter."

"I appreciate that," Clara said, reaching over to touch the old colonel's hand. "It is never easy to talk about these things."

"If Susan O'Harris had been alive in 1913 I would have handed her head on a platter to you as a killer. She was a demon if ever I saw one. She killed them all with her wickedness. She had the markings of a murderess, not dear Flo."

"I am afraid not everything is so clear cut," Clara sighed.

"Thank you for coming Miss Fitzgerald, I'm sure eventually I shall feel I did the right thing telling you all this."

"I can assure you, you did."

"If you don't mind, I think I shall retire to my home," the colonel stood stiffly. "I could do with a rest."

Clara nodded.

"Take care Colonel Brandt."

"You too, my dear, and, if possible, find out the truth about Goddard's death."

"I shall certainly try."

Chapter Fifteen

Arriving at home, Clara found her thoughts turning to a warm cup of tea and a chance to sit down quietly and muse on everything she had been told. She entered the house and made her way to the kitchen, intending to disturb the household as little as possible, but found Annie there cleaning pots.

"Annie? Surely this is your afternoon off?"

"The pots needed scrubbing."

Clara glanced at the neat lines of copper pots along the walls, most were unused these days and certainly did not require the intense cleaning Annie was now giving them.

"I thought I would make myself a cup of tea, shall I make you one," Clara said, carefully snatching up the big metal kettle before Annie could protest and insist on making it herself.

"If you like," Annie said instead, not looking from her work.

Clara filled the kettle at the big kitchen pump, a left over from the Victorian days of the house and glanced over at the maid at the sink. Something was wrong, she could sense it. She put the kettle on the stove to boil and wandered over to the window where the sink stood and surreptitiously observed her maid and friend.

"I have been chatting with Colonel Brandt, poor man seems very lonely," she remarked as a distraction.

"I don't think I know him," Annie answered blithely, then she gave a slight sniff.

"He was to do with the O'Harris family. Now they were a curious bunch, I really don't know what to make of them."

"I can't say myself," Annie said, seeming uninterested in the entire conversation.

"Tommy was supposed to be doing some research for me, did you take him out?"

Annie scraped even harder at the spotlessly clean pan.

"I did."

"Annie, is something the matter?"

The scrubbing brush paused.

"Why would you say that, miss?"

"Because of this frenzied cleaning and your unusual lack of conversation and also the fact you have clearly been crying."

Annie turned to face her mistress, and now it was obvious to see her eyes were puffy and red.

"I don't care to talk about it."

"Yet I do, I don't like seeing you so upset. So, what is it?"

Annie dumped the pan in the sink and grabbed up a tea towel to dry her wet hands.

"It ain't nothing."

"Then it must be something," Clara said calmly. "Unless you want to rephrase that double negative."

Annie glared at her, a look that took Clara quite by surprise and made her hesitate.

"Is it something I have done?"

"No, don't be silly," Annie bustled away as the kettle began to sing.

"Well, we can't have this, Annie. I am your friend first and foremost and I can't bear seeing you so miserable. What has happened?"

Annie fussed with a China teapot, measuring out carefully procured tea leaves.

"You won't tell me? Then I must guess," Clara took a seat at the kitchen table. "Let me see, have you argued with someone?"

Annie gave a strange huff and turned aside.

"So, an argument. With whom? Well, you say not me, and I don't recall arguing with you anyway. Was it that boy in the butchers who you can't abide?"

"Just because a lad doesn't know how to cut a joint of meat right, don't mean I will be shedding tears over it!" Annie snapped.

"Then it is something more personal?" Clara let the question hang in the air for a moment, "There is only one thing I can think of that would mean that much to you Annie. What is the problem between you and Tommy?"

Annie stormed over to the table and thudded down the teapot, then she sank into a chair and wiped furiously at her teary eyes.

"It ain't right to talk of it to you, you being his sister and all."

"Nonsense, I am the best person to talk to. I am less likely than anyone else to take his side," Clara smiled lightly.

"I'm not saying anything," Annie insisted, she poured out a cup of tea that splashed over the rim of the cup.

"You two really have fallen out?" Clara shook her head, "I was only gone a short while!"

Annie said nothing but drank shakily from her cup. Clara decided it was time to deal with the other side of this argument.

Tommy was in his usual spot at the parlour table going through the diaries of Florence O'Harris once again. He didn't look up as Clara entered.

"What nonsense have you two been arguing about?" Clara asked immediately.

She sat down in the nearest armchair and scowled at him. Tommy refused to meet her eye.

"Annie surely told you," he said casually.

"Annie is in a fine temper. I've never known her spill a cup of tea before. I can only imagine what you have done to upset her so."

"That's it, blame me instantly," Tommy responded gruffly.

"Then Annie has caused this?"

Tommy hunkered down over the diaries a little more.

"You are pinning me into a corner. It's a silly thing anyway, Annie has thrown it all out of proportion."

"Thrown what out of proportion?"

Tommy grumbled something under his breath, then he looked at his sister.

"While you were out Captain O'Harris visited."

"Did you apologise for my absence?"

"Yes, though he wasn't entirely looking for you. I mean he *was* looking for you, because he really rather likes you, old girl. Had you noticed?"

"Don't change the subject," Clara interjected sternly.

"Fine. He came, though it may surprise you, to see me in fact."

Clara was now truly curious.

"What did you talk about?"

"Aeroplanes. The captain wanted to talk about aviation and knew I was interested. Besides, I am about the only person in Brighton with any knowledge on the subject. Aside from you, of course, but then you aren't exactly the usual lady about town."

"As you are my brother, I shall accept that as a compliment, and stop trying to distract me."

Tommy rolled his eyes.

"O'Harris has his mind set on breaking the Atlantic crossing record, he is pretty confident on the matter and having sat in the *Buzzard* I can see why. She is a fine plane. You should try her one day."

"Or not," Clara said. "This hardly seems cause for an argument with Annie."

"No, that's because I am beating about the bush," Tommy frowned. "The captain's co-pilot has dropped out of the venture. Broke his arm falling off his horse last week and won't be fit any time soon. Without a co-pilot the matter is really at an end."

Clara felt a pang of relief. Had it really bothered her that much that Captain O'Harris would be flying across the Atlantic? She tried to shake the thought, but she couldn't help but feel it was better for him to remain grounded.

"He needs a new co-pilot," Tommy continued. "Not necessarily an experienced person, he could train him up. Just someone a bit mechanically minded and eager. He has sent telegrams to old friends, but no one is about and then it occurred to him that there was someone to hand he could ask."

Clara felt her relief turn to dread.

"He asked me to be his co-pilot," Tommy finished uneasily.

Clara instantly wanted to snap at him, to tell him it was so idiotic a suggestion he shouldn't even contemplate it, but clearly that was what Annie had done and Clara knew how stubborn her brother was. She kept her temper.

"Doesn't a plane have foot pedals?" She asked cautiously.

"I thought that, apparently it is mostly hand controls but with a long pedal under the feet for rudder adjustments. I told him an old crock like me couldn't do it, but he reckons I could if I just set my mind to it. I don't think he is the sort of fellow who believes anything

FLIGHT OF FANCY

is impossible. And he said, should it prove tricky, he was certain he could have some sort of special arrangement set up, so the rudder was operated by hand."

"You've considered this then?"

Tommy met and held his sister's gaze.

"It's a once in a lifetime opportunity Clara," his tone was suddenly serious. "Let's be straight with each other. What options have I for much of a life now? I can't even ride a bicycle for crying out loud. If the man thinks I can fly, well, perhaps I should at least try. I sat in that plane Clara, and I was alive again, my blood pumping in my head, my body tingling. It didn't matter about my legs then. I was free."

Clara kept as calm as she could to reply.

"I understand, I really do. You want to prove to yourself you are still the person you once were."

"No, you *don't* understand Clara," Tommy looked miserable. "I'll never be the person I was before the war again, too much has happened. But... look, for once I would like the world to see me not as poor Tommy Fitzgerald who came home a cripple, but Tommy Fitzgerald who braved the Atlantic. For once I want their admiration not their pity. For once I want to be the object of envy to my friends, rather than the other way around."

"And you will sacrifice all you have got for that moment of admiration and glory?"

"Yes! What have I here anyway?"

Clara was silent a moment, she let his own words sink into him, perhaps he really didn't know what he had, what was right under his nose.

"Don't be so dense Tommy."

Tommy closed his eyes. For a moment he seemed to sink into his thoughts, then he looked up.

"This could be my last chance."

"For what? A flash in the pan adventure? Next year O'Harris' flight will be old news. Someone will have done something different or have broken his record. Then your moment of glory will be another annotation in some sporting history book. You need to be pretty damn sure you are prepared to sacrifice a lifetime with Annie for that."

Tommy had clearly not expected her to be so blunt. He looked a little stunned at her words.

"Annie will be here when I get back."

"If you get back Tommy, nothing is guaranteed once you get in that plane. And I am not as confident as you are that she will be waiting."

"You are trying to put me off! It is my life to do with as I please!"

"Yes, I know," Clara bit her tongue, "But all our lives touch others and we have to make our decisions based on more than our own desires. Annie thinks the world of you, but she has suffered too much loss in her short life to be able to deal with this adventure of yours easily."

"Really, you are both making such a fuss."

"Take a moment to look at things from her perspective. Annie lost her entire family in the war, she had no one until I stumbled on her. Now her life revolves around me and you, but mainly you. If you get in that plane you may die, in fact the odds are probably stacked against you somewhat…"

"You are talking nonsense."

"Did captain O'Harris tell you of his friend who just died while flying over the Arctic?"

Tommy didn't answer, O'Harris had not.

"Annie is hurt inside in a way both of us barely understand. If you fly with O'Harris it will scare the life out of her in case you are lost. I am not sure she could stand losing you and I know she will find it hard to forgive you for risking your life for an adventure."

"Speak bluntly why don't you?" Tommy snapped.

"No one will stop you getting in that plane Tommy if you feel you must," Clara said calmly. "But you need to be aware of what you may be giving up for your flight of fancy."

"Annie will be here when I come back," Tommy said stubbornly.

"Perhaps she will," Clara shrugged. "Just as long as you are prepared to take the chance she might not be."

Tommy clenched his fists. He was churning inside with so many emotions it pained him. He wanted to fly, to do something that an ordinary man could, but he hardly dared admit that fear followed that desire and also guilt. He knew how worried Annie and Clara would be if he flew with O'Harris. The captain had been blunt about the risks, had said it was only fair to be as honest as possible on the matter. There were many dangers; engine failure, damage to the plane, bad weather, fatigue, illness. A lot of things could ruin a flight, but deaths were not as frequent as people feared, or so O'Harris swore.

But this was his life and Tommy ultimately had the freedom to do as he wished. What man would wish to stay on the ground when the opportunity presented itself to soar high?

"I understand now why Annie is so upset," Clara mused. "I shan't say anymore on the matter. It is your decision."

"You would rather I didn't fly," Tommy stated.

"In the end it is not my choice. I shall be worried about you if you do, of course."

"This could be my last chance..."

"At what?"

Tommy couldn't explain, but at the back of his mind was this strange knot of anxiety that if he refused now, he would regret it all his life.

Chapter Sixteen

The nameplate on the wall read Dr Cutt; Clara paused a moment to smile then rang the bell. A prim woman in a long apron answered and stared at the woman on her step.

"You're not a regular."

"I am afraid not, but I do have an appointment to see Dr Cutt."

"It's Wednesday afternoon, Dr Cutt doesn't see patients on a Wednesday afternoon unless it's an emergency."

"Ah, but I am not a patient. Clara fumbled in her bag and found a business card; she handed it to the woman who almost crossed her eyes trying to read it.

"I haven't my glasses on," she said after trying to focus on the card at various distances. "What does it say."

"Miss Clara Fitzgerald," Clara answered, "I am a visitor, and I rang earlier to arrange an appointment with the good doctor."

"So, you're not sick?"

"Hardly," Clara considered herself robust enough to avoid visiting doctors normally. She had little time for the medicines and tinctures they dispensed randomly.

"I'll go see if Dr Cutt is ready for you. Step into the hall," the woman backed away, still trying to read the card, and left Clara in a small hallway while she went to check with Dr Cutt.

Clara noted the door to her left marked 'waiting room' and the faint odour of iodine and bleach. Each smell conjured up visions of the hospital she had helped in during the war and brought back unpleasant visions of the terrible injuries people had sustained in bombardments by the Germans. She had seen far too many die during her time there, and the smell of chemicals now brought a sick feeling to her stomach.

She was relieved when the woman returned and escorted her to a room at the back of the house, distant enough from the surgery to not be penetrated by the medical aromas. Dr Cutt was sat in a pleasant garden room enjoying the afternoon sunshine while he clipped a newspaper article from the day's paper. He stood as Clara entered and offered his hand.

"Dr Josiah Cutt."

Dr Cutt was not a day younger than eighty, but sprightly and keen, with a brightness to his eyes, semi-masked by a pair of old spectacles. He was dressed in a tweed suit and a crisp white shirt, his collar ornamented with a bowtie. He offered Clara a seat and smiled as he slipped back into his own.

"On Wednesday afternoons I catch up with the news," he motioned to the paper on the table and several others on the floor with pink, clean hands. "I cut out anything of a medical nature that interests me and keep it in my scrapbooks. Surprising how often it comes in handy."

"I can imagine," Clara noted several other scrapbooks arranged on a bookcase near the fire.

"I think it important to keep a close note on my dealings with patients. One can't rely entirely on the memory, and one never knows when a rare case may crop up and a little scrap of knowledge from the past might prove useful."

He carefully moved his papers to one side.

"I told my housekeeper to bring in the tea things, I know it is a tad early, but I hope it shall not matter."

"Not at all," Clara smiled, suddenly recalling she had missed lunch yet again. "I do apologise for interrupting your afternoon off."

"Oh nonsense," Dr Cutt smiled broadly. "A visitor is hardly an interruption, unless it is Mr Henry complaining about his gout again. I keep explaining to him it cannot be so bad if he can walk a mile to me to moan about it."

"I am sure he pays full heed," Clara laughed.

"Yes, well, one finds being an old doctor, one's patients tend to be on the old side too. I have men under my care I first saw as boys who now look older and dodderier than I do. Sometimes I wonder when my turn will come to feel my age."

"As long as you keep working, probably never."

"Too true, now Miss Fitzgerald, if I recall rightly you wanted to ask me about a patient who died some years ago. By the way, are you the same Miss Fitzgerald who solved the murder of Mrs Greengage?"

Clara was flattered he had heard of her.

"Indeed, I am."

"I once paid a house call on her husband you know," Dr Cutt rubbed at his chin thoughtfully. "Worst case of shellshock I had seen in a while. He couldn't leave the house at all. It was very hard on them both."

"Shellshock?"

"Are you not aware of the condition?"

"I have never heard the term."

"Well, I suppose that would be right enough, the authorities have kept it most quiet from the public. Shellshock is a term for a nervous disorder resulting from being in the war," Dr Cutt tapped his fingers on the table unconsciously. "It comes in many forms, but most usual is that a man just breaks. One moment he seems quite fine, the next he is a gibbering wreck. It's said to be caused by the constant shelling that took place during the war, it drives a man slowly insane by the noise alone. I read all I could on it, and I have seen a fair few cases in Brighton."

"My brother was taken badly during the war," Clara admitted. "He was shot in the legs and was a long time recovering, but he was kept in the military hospital even longer because he could become quite irrational. He would lose his temper over nothing and some days he was so morose and withdrawn I hardly felt he knew I was there."

"Shellshock to be certain."

Clara was toying with the edge of the tablecloth, remembering something Tommy's doctors had once said.

"Could shell-shock cause a person to forget how to do something, such as walk?"

Dr Cutt took a moment to answer.

"I suppose, I've seen all manner of odd behaviour caused by it."

"You see my brother, Thomas Fitzgerald, he hasn't walked since he was injured, but the doctors tell us he should be able to. There is no damage they can see that could cause him to remain crippled. Sometimes, when he is half-asleep say, you can get him to stand and walk a little. It is almost as though when his brain is not concentrating, he can move his legs, but as soon as he thinks about it, he can't."

"That is very interesting," Dr Cutt meant what he said, he was developing a theory on shellshock and the best means of helping sufferers. "Has he seen anyone recently?"

"Not since he left the hospital."

"And no one ever mentioned a diagnosis of shellshock to you?"

Clara shook her head.

"I would be happy to meet your brother and see for myself his problem, I have been working on a paper about the condition in collaboration with a psychiatric specialist in Edinburgh. We regularly discuss cases, but we have not come across one where a man *thinks* he can't walk when he *can*. Do you think he would meet me for a chat?"

"I make no promises," Clara knew her brother had an aversion to doctors. "But I shall ask him."

"Thank you, Miss Fitzgerald, ah, I do hear the tea things coming."

As he spoke there was a rattling noise in the hallway and Dr Cutt's housekeeper entered with a tray laden with teapot, sandwiches, cake, and cups. She deposited it on the table and started pouring out tea while the doctor continued.

"Now, what was it you wished to see me about? An old patient of mine I believe?"

"Yes, I am looking into the death of Goddard O'Harris."

"Ah, yes, the man who just up and vanished."

"Precisely," Clara took the cup she was handed and thanked the housekeeper. "I have been given some conflicting information as to his state of health before his death."

"Really?"

"Yes, it has been suggested to me he was gravely ill. A wasting disease. I asked around and discovered you became his doctor after the death of Dr Brandt."

"That is true," Dr Cutt took a deep sip of his tea as his housekeeper withdrew, then stood up and went to a brown cabinet. "I keep my old patient files in here."

He spent several moments sorting through several bundles of papers that filled the large cabinet. Clara sipped patiently at her hot tea and wondered what stories were hidden away in those files. She told herself off for being so nosy.

"This is the one," Dr Cutt brought over a pale brown cardboard folder and laid it on the table. "Goddard O'Harris was my patient for over twenty years before his death. Dr Brandt retired in 1888, I believe, and handed his patients on to me. Sadly, he was not a well man and died shortly after. I have his notes as well, which means I have a medical record for Goddard O'Harris' entire life just about."

Dr Cutt opened the folder which contained several pages covered with a thin, spidery handwriting, that quite baffled Clara's abilities to decipher it.

"He was relatively healthy. Suffered an injury to the hip while in the army and it caused him lasting problems. His notes say it was probably caused by poor treatment of the wound at the time, it never quite healed and he had arthritis in his hips and legs from the time I knew him."

"But nothing life-threatening?"

"From his hip? No, no," Dr Cutt flicked through his papers. "He did have a weak heart. I remember that now. I warned him to be wary of sudden excitement, but he was not the sort of man to work himself into a temper, so I was hardly worried."

"Was his heart condition because of his time in the army?"

"No, I would say it was hereditary. I did once enquire whether his family had been known for heart problems and he recalled his mother having palpitations and his grandfather had chest pains quite often after walking or riding. It says it all here in my notes, I try to be thorough. Mind you, it never stopped any of them from living a full life."

"Nothing about a wasting disease?"

Dr Cutt examined his notes a little more thoroughly.

"No, not a mention. I saw Goddard two weeks before his death and aside from his usual complaints he was as fit as a fiddle. He wanted to know if I thought it would be all right for him to ride in the hunt that winter, he always asked. I suspect his wife insisted. She felt better if I had given him the all-clear."

Clara reflected on yet another instance of Florence's concern for her husband.

"It was rather odd how he died," Dr Cutt, closed the file and considered carefully. "I mean, from a professional point of view I would say his heart gave out. It was due, anyway."

"That would be quick?"

"It can be. But I suppose your interest is why, if the death was natural, did someone move the body?"

Clara smiled at the observant doctor.

"It is troubling, would you not say."

"Yes, and I have been through it in my mind for, shall we say a less sinister motive than hiding up a murder. For instance, I wondered whether there was perhaps some money involved, say an insurance policy that would not pay out if it could be proved his death was caused by a pre-existing condition such as his heart. But I never heard of anything of the sort and really what would the O'Harrises need with life insurance?"

"Again, and again, I can find no logical reason for removing the body other than murder or, at least, presumed murder," Clara agreed.

"I'm sorry I wasn't more help," sighed the doctor, he picked up a plate of sandwiches and offered her one.

"I was really only trying to tie up loose ends," Clara answered. "I seem to be going around and around in circles."

"No one ever solved the case at the time, I doubt you will now, but it is good to see someone making the effort."

"Thank you, but I have a little more confidence in myself," Clara assured him. "There is a logical solution to everything."

"Indeed, well do your best and please feel free to send your brother to me."

"Thank you, Dr Cutt, I shall do just that."

Chapter Seventeen

Clara found herself uncertain what to do when she left the doctor's house. It was far from usual for her to be caught in indecision, but she found she was struggling to know what her next move should be.

In the end she wandered into the High Street and stared idly into a window or two before her eye fell on Bankes' Photographic Studio. She couldn't explain what made her pause or what caused the feeling of guilt inside her. All she knew was the next instance she had an impulse to buy two jam tarts from the bakery and take them over in a neat white paper bag to the business premises of Oliver Bankes.

Oliver was tucked away in his laboratory mixing up a new developing solution he was experimenting with when Clara appeared. He had just discovered that his latest concoction ate paper and was coughing in a cloud of chemical smoke.

For a moment Clara was stunned as Oliver stood blithely wafting smoke from his face, while he made gagging sounds, apparently oblivious to how dangerous the chemicals might be. She reacted quickly, reaching out and grabbing his arm and dragging him into the hallway. She escorted him to his office, thrust him into a chair and found a glass full of water among the debris on his desk. She gave it to him and made him drink some. Slowly Oliver stopped choking and he grinned at her.

"Clara, dear girl."

"You just about killed yourself," Clara said crossly, wondering why she was suddenly so angry.

"Neither of the chemicals are all that harmful, I think," Oliver frowned.

"But in combination?"

Oliver gave a shrug and his smile returned.

"It did make a good puff of smoke."

Clara shook her head.

"Why is it every man I encounter seems determined to do away with himself at the slightest opportunity?"

"I say! I was only mixing up a new formula for my developing fluid. I have in mind a means for getting a darker image if I can just get the solution right."

"And in the meantime, you will choke to death?"

Oliver gave a hoarse cough.

"I'm sure it was harmless. Say, what do I owe the pleasure?"

Clara picked up the paper bag and passed it over.

"For some unfathomable reason I felt like popping in and visiting."

Oliver peeped in the bag and saw the jam tarts.

"Lovely! Just could do with an afternoon pick-me-up. Do you care for a plate? I might be able to find one…"

Both their eyes trailed to the heaped-up desk, the papers in disarray, dirty crockery stacked in heaps, poorly developed photographs scattered across the top.

"I think I can manage."

"As you can see, I am not terribly fussed about crumbs," Oliver had the decency to look abashed at the state of his office as he handed over a jam tart. "I bet you were after looking at some photos of the old O'Harris house?"

In fact, it had not crossed Clara's mind, but Oliver was already getting up and searching through one of his great wooden filing cabinets while he munched on the tart.

"Father probably took some, he took lots of different things," Oliver fudged through over-stuffed drawers. "Any closer to a solution?"

"No, not really," Clara looked around the office, noting the dying geranium on the windowsill and resisting the urge to water it.

"Ah, damn it, I can't find them," Oliver cursed, closing one filing cabinet and heading for another.

"It doesn't matter."

"But you came all this way just to see them!"

"No, I didn't."

They paused. Clara realised she was blushing a second after Oliver had turned around to look at her with an expression of surprise and delight.

"I mean..." Clara fumbled, "I was in the High Street and last time I was a touch rude and... I thought I might make amends."

Oliver shoved closed the drawers of the cabinet and came back towards her.

"You came just to visit?"

"Yes, well, I suppose..."

"I thought you were still on the O'Harris mystery."

"I am, but I don't spend *all* my time on it. Just most," Clara found the embarrassment lifting. "Besides, someone has to turn up and pull you out of a gas cloud, don't they?"

"I'll try and gas myself more often then, if it brings you running."

"Please don't," Clara took a bite of her tart, grateful for the distraction. "I have enough with my brother and his adventures."

"Tommy? What is he up to?"

"He has this notion in his head he can be a co-pilot for Captain O'Harris on his next flight. They both have it planned."

"Flying?" Oliver shuddered at the idea, planes held as much allure for him as a muddy ditch, "Really? And you will let him?"

"It's not up to me, he has his own life and, well, he can lead it as he chooses. I have voiced my thoughts but if he really wants to do it, what right do I have to stop him?"

Clara abruptly looked so miserable Oliver reached out his hand and touched hers.

"I could have a word with him?"

"Thanks, all the same, but you can't say more than I have, and he will know I sent you and I would hate that."

"Then talk to O'Harris, tell him not to take Tommy!"

"O'Harris is stubborn as a mule and certainly would not listen to me."

"I doubt that," Oliver smiled sadly. "He is rather taken by you, can't you tell?"

Clara could tell and she had to admit she had been flattered by his attention, but she also knew he was a man who would put his spirit of adventure and lust for freedom before anything else.

"He still would not listen to me."

"Then what will you do?"

That was the question that Clara had no idea how to answer.

"I suppose I shall carry on as usual," She ate a corner of the tart, the jam still slightly under-sweetened and bitter tasting. When would sugar become a staple again? "Could we talk of something else?"

"The O'Harris murder?"

"No, something other than that."

"All right let me show you my latest photographs," Oliver led Clara back through to his laboratory full of enthusiasm. "I've been experimenting with light and dark. That is why I am trying to fix a better developing solution. If I can get really dark shadows, I can take my pictures the next step."

He grabbed a picture off a string hanging from the ceiling. It showed an image of a small bridge over a stream, each of the bridge railings heavily contrasted against the bright sky.

"You see this one, why this was near perfect. The shadows are so deep you feel you can fall into them and look how they make the reflection in the water stand out. And this one..." He grabbed a photo of an old cartwheel propped against a wall, "See how every spoke casts this dark shadow? You feel you could pick it up. Compare it to a normal photo and you can see the difference, the shadows, well they just 'pop'."

"Pop?"

"This could be a whole new way with photography. Imagine, Clara, if we could make photography a form of art rather than just a way of recording people and events. If photos were hung in galleries next to old masters and admired in the same way, imagine!"

Clara enjoyed his enthusiasm; it bubbled over and was highly infectious.

"Perhaps one day."

"But first we have to perfect the art of taking a picture. I have no time for these photographers who touch up their shots afterwards, painting in what they actually wanted. No, I want to capture what my eye sees, and I want it to be purely an act of photography."

"You seem to be on the right track."

"Well yes, but, and here I really must curse my own slap-dash ways. I failed to write down the formula for the solution that made these images and now I simply can't remember it," Oliver pegged the photos back onto the string and turned to his trays and chemicals. "I can remember the first step, but it is the amount of the later components that flummoxes me. I'm sure it was three drops..."

"Oliver, you are not mixing that now?"

There was a sudden snap and a new waft of pungent gas erupted from the dish Oliver was standing before. Clara watched in horror as he took a pace back and then collapsed. She rushed to him and found he was unconscious.

"Oliver!" She slapped his cheek, slowly his eyes fluttered open.

"That quite took my breath away!" He rose himself on his elbows, "Did I faint?"

"Don't you dare do that again! These chemicals are dangerous, that is twice you have nearly gassed yourself!"

"But I only fainted," Oliver protested. "I'm sure that shouldn't have happened anyway, I'm starting to think some of my supplies are contaminated."

"One minute you were there and the next you were gone," Clara involuntarily shivered. "It was quite horrid."

"Funny how a gas can do that," Oliver said, his joviality at odds with Clara's concern. "I just took a sniff and bang I was flat on the floor. I never even realised."

Clara pulled him to his feet.

"At least, if you must dabble with these things, do it outside in the fresh air!"

"Yes," Oliver was more amenable now he was up and noting that his head was thumping hard. "I think I might have to lie down for a bit, that gave me one shocker of a headache."

Clara sighed.

"You have an apartment upstairs?"

"I do."

"Then go get some rest and I will shut your shop for you. Have you a spare key."

Oliver offered some vague directions to a spare key beneath the counter. His grin had returned by the time he headed for the stairs, idly rubbing his head.

Clara was of the opinion mankind was hopelessly inept and determined to make themselves extinct as she fished out the key and left the shop. The spring sun was shining, but it was still cold as she set out for home. She pulled on her gloves. A thought was nagging at the back of her mind, it had been since she had helped Oliver, but she had been too busy to notice.

She let her mind go blank as she walked, hoping this would draw out the errant thought. What was it that was bothering her? She waved to a friend and tried to think about supper and whether Annie had forgiven Tommy yet, but something still niggled at the back of her mind. It was something to do with the gas Oliver had created. Was it lingering fear?

She turned off West Street and concentrated on her way home. Boys were playing in the road, dodging horses and carts and the odd motor car. She watched them without seeing. The thought was starting to form, but if she reached out too soon it would slip from her. She watched a pigeon heading for its nest with a mouthful of twigs and slowly wondered if the doves would roost in her pear tree again. She turned a corner and suddenly it was bang there before her eyes, so obvious she could have slapped herself.

Clara hurried home, was breathless when she arrived and let herself in. She went straight to Tommy.

"Gas Tommy! But it could have been gas!"

Tommy looked at her aghast, then he slowly turned the book he was reading towards her.

"I was just thinking the same, more specifically arsine gas."

Chapter Eighteen

The book was about early experiments into using gas in warfare and it had been written by Goddard O'Harris.

"The bulk of the book is about how throughout history new weapons have been developed, but there is a whole chapter about gas weapons. All the time I was reading it I was thinking that if you wanted the perfect murder weapon this would be it. Pick the right gas and there would be no marks on the body and no sign of what occurred, and it is quick," Tommy flipped a page. "There is a whole section here on arsine gas, it's a form of arsenic but it is highly deadly. Workmen in certain industries where white arsenic is a by-product used to stumble upon pockets of arsine gas. It was instantly fatal, and men just dropped down dead. Goddard mentioned how it was considered as a humane gas for use in war, but delivering it was the problem and other gases found favour instead."

Tommy felt violently sick.

"I've seen lads choked by gas in the trenches. The lucky ones died immediately, the unlucky ones got took to the hospital and suffered days of torment before they passed. Some of the stuff they threw at us rots you from the inside out," Tommy had to stop, the images were too strong in his mind. "Seeing it so calmly written about in a book turns my stomach. Goddard wasn't just describing it; he was advocating it!"

Clara took the book and read a few paragraphs, then she placed it down and was silent.

"This is the first clue we have had to point to a murder weapon," Tommy continued. "It's not conclusive, but what else have we got."

"It had to be something like this, or a poison. Did you look up fast acting poisons?"

"Yes, but with little luck. To kill a person instantly with a poison you would need a huge dose and delivering it would be difficult. The person would be liable to notice the taste or have a dramatic reaction."

"But arsine gas?"

"Goddard states it is almost odour-less, is colour-less and is denser than air, which is essential when using gas as a weapon. It is also lethal in very small doses. Its downside is that it is highly flammable. It usually occurs when material containing arsenic is mixed with arsenic-free zinc and dissolved with sulphuric acid. Arsine gas is given off and can be quite hazardous to chemists."

"So how could it be delivered to Goddard?"

"That, I don't know. A hidden canister perhaps?"

"This is almost unthinkable," Clara stared at the page. "But Goddard wrote of it, could he have... No, I don't have a reason for suicide. If he had been dying it might have been different but there was nothing wrong with Goddard except for a bad heart."

"This mystery stunk of murder from the start."

"I agree, but the murderer had to have a fair amount of chemical knowledge to develop his weapon, and you have to admit it was worth it. The crime has gone unsolved these last ten years."

They sat in silence for a while. The mantel clock ticked towards five o'clock and distantly the clinking of crockery suggested Annie was laying the table.

"She hasn't said a word to me all day," Tommy sighed.

Clara made no response, even if it did take all her effort to bite her tongue.

"I wish she could be more understanding," Tommy pushed for a reaction, but his sister would not give him the satisfaction. "Perhaps that is why O'Harris has no girl."

"O'Harris is very lonely," Clara said quietly. "That is something to bear in mind."

"Because he flies?"

"I did not mean that. Just, he sees the world differently to you and me," Clara caught her brother's eyes and tried to impress upon him her words, but she would not spell it out for him, not again.

"Oh, while you were out a letter was delivered," Tommy wheeled himself to the mantelpiece and retrieved an envelope.

It bore Clara's name in a poor hand, but no address. The envelope was slightly dirty. Clara opened it and pulled out a sheet of paper, marked at the edges with dirty fingerprints. There was only one sentence on the paper.

"No good comes of digging up the past!"

"Warning no.2," Clara waved the note at Tommy.

"You do attract them Clara, last case it was a stalker this one threatening letters."

"I think I'm close Tommy," Clara smiled. "I think I have the killer on the run."

Tommy looked worried.

"You talk of me taking risks Clara, but you are getting threats and do nothing about it but smile and say it proves you are right. What if this killer tries to put you out of the way?"

"Don't be so dramatic," Clara tutted. "That sort of thing only occurs in books."

"I still think you need to be careful."

"Well, remind me of that when you get in O'Harris' plane," Clara said pointedly.

Tommy scowled, but there was no point in arguing further.

When Clara found her way to Belgrave Street the next morning she was in fine spirits. She finally felt on course and the solution to this riddle seemed within reach. The last few pieces needed to fall into place and then she would have her answer. It was so exciting she felt a spring in her step, and it almost distracted her from thoughts of Tommy taking to the skies. O'Harris had printed an announcement in the paper that morning that the weather looked promising for an attempt at the record next weekend. Clara's heart had jolted at the words. She hid the paper from Annie, but she would know sooner or later.

Down Belgrave Street lived Owen Clarence the builder who had constructed the garage next to the O'Harris house. The road was lined with small terraces, some in serious need of a builder's attention. Dark-eyed women watched her from doorways as she trotted past in her smart jacket and heels. Clara refused to be intimidated, even when a dirty pair of boys started following her. She turned on them abruptly and told them to leave her alone. She must have seemed particularly forceful that morning because they both scampered away.

Even so, she was glad to find Clarence's house at last and be let in.

"Good morning, Mr Clarence, I'm glad I caught you in."

"Ah, well you would do, my back is playing up again," Mr Clarence was in his fifties with grey hair. He shuffled uneasily into a parlour and pointed out a seat to Clara. Stretching out his back painfully he asked if she would care for a cup of tea.

"Please don't put yourself out," Clara responded.

Mr Clarence nodded. With great care he lowered himself into a high-backed armchair, a grimace of discomfort scuttling across his face.

"What did you do to it?" Clara asked sympathetically.

"Usual thing, trying to lift more than I should. I'm short-handed, that's the trouble of it. Hardly any fit lads in the area and the ones that are, are trying to look for better work than being a labourer. That war gave 'em all airs and graces, I tell you! Lads who before the war would have been glad to get into the building trade, now they turn their noses up and say as they will try and get something better."

Mr Clarence eased his aching back with a cushion.

"It is most unfortunate," Clara said. "Is there nothing the doctor can give you?"

Mr Clarence waved a hand disparagingly.

"Don't start me on doctors miss. What they know ain't worth tuppence, but anyhow, what was it you called about? I ain't exactly taking on work at the moment."

"Oh, it isn't like that," Clara answered. "I am making enquiries on the behalf of Captain O'Harris."

"The pilot fellow? Thinks he can cross the Atlantic in that little wooden box of his?"

"That would be him." Clara agreed, her mind uncomfortably turning over the words 'little wooden box,' "I am helping him to solve an old family mystery and I was told by someone you might be able to help."

"By whom?"

"Oh, a painter I believe. It was a chance conversation."

Mr Clarence looked uncertain, clearly wondering if some of his old building work was about to come into question.

"This has nothing to do with your integrity as a craftsman," Clara buttered him up. "In fact, it has more to do with someone disturbing your work. I am talking about the garage or barn you built for Goddard O'Harris just over ten years ago."

Mr Clarence's eyes lit up.

"I remember that!"

"Do you also remember remarking that the footings of your project were disturbed?"

Mr Clarence hesitated. A lot of time had passed since 1913 and a lot of building projects too. He had seen a daughter married and a son go to war, welcomed home his first grandchild, and spent far more time than he would care to think about repairing and demolishing bomb-damaged Brighton. Lots of memories had been made and forgotten, but a thing like the O'Harris disappearance, that stuck in your brain.

"I recall there were all manner of rumours about where the body went to."

"Yes?"

"I can't think who first suggested the footings would make a good grave. One of the workmen, I guess. It weren't me, I know that, I never gave it much interest once I knew Mrs O'Harris could keep paying us."

"But once you did think of it?"

"I can't be certain, but one morning I looked at the foundations we had just dug and filled. We dug them and filled 'em day after O'Harris died. Well, I looked at 'em and I thought to myself something funny is going on here. They were all disturbed, there were splashes of concrete all on the side of the trench, and not just the splashes you make filling the things. These were big splashes, as though someone had been messing about in the concrete and slopped some over the sides. Then I looked a bit more and I thought to myself, well I don't know but that concrete looks higher than I recall. You see it weren't just a splash, but the concrete had over-filled the trench and slopped over. It was messy and I didn't like it. I knew I hadn't left it that way."

Clara realised she hadn't breathed for a moment or two.

"What could have caused that Mr Clarence? Aside from you over-filling it?"

"I didn't over-fill it, of that I can assure you."

"I believe you, but what would have caused it?"

Mr Clarence thought silently for a while again.

"Only one way I can see it happening. Someone put something in the concrete that caused it to splash over the sides. They dropped it in, yes, that's how I would describe it."

Clara thought her heart was pounding in excitement. Could it be she had located the body of Goddard O'Harris?

"Precisely Mr Clarence which foundation trench are we referring to?"

"The East trench, southern end. Perhaps I should have done something then? Oh well, too late now."

Clara was up and grabbing her handbag.

"It is never too late Mr Clarence. Thank you for the chat, I do hope your back feels better soon." Clara pulled on her hat, "No, don't get up, I'll let myself out!"

She flew away with renewed determination. Mr Clarence watched her curiously and wondered if the Goddard O'Harris mystery was about to be unravelled.

Chapter Nineteen

"The foundations?"

Captain O'Harris looked sick to his stomach after hearing Clara's revelations.

"We have to dig them up."

He and Clara were stood before the garage staring at the wide doors set into the Southern side.

"It will be a lot of work," O'Harris answered reluctantly.

"Your uncle could be lying down there."

O'Harris scratched at his ear.

"I suppose if they just dismantled this section, it would be feasible. I can arrange it for sure," O'Harris sighed. "Clara, I'm really worried you are building a case for my aunt to be a murderer."

"I am not," Clara reached out for his sleeve, "Now, there will be no work done today so why don't we discuss that list of servants?"

As she spoke the first drops of a heavy spring rain shower fell on them. O'Harris glanced at *Buzzard*, who he had been cleaning as Clara arrived.

"Very well. Go into the drawing room, I need to get the old girl under cover."

With that they went their separate ways.

Clara was almost overwhelmed with elation. She was close to certain that when the concrete under O'Harris' garage was picked away it would reveal the corpse of unfortunate Goddard. Better still, she felt she was finally inching towards the way he died. Arsine gas had such potential, but if it were the cause, it also could only have been used by a limited number of individuals – those who had a passing knowledge of chemistry. Even so, she had to keep an open mind. Nothing was true until it was proved and there still could be other possibilities. It just felt as though she was unerringly drawing towards the murderer.

O'Harris appeared in the doorway rubbing his hands on a cloth.

"I've asked the housekeeper to call a builder and arrange for the demolishing of the garage," O'Harris was sullen. "I hope you are right about this Clara."

"Do you doubt my conclusions?"

He threw the cloth aside.

"Not as such, I mean they are logical. But to think of him lying there in a place I walk past every morning... It is simply horrible."

"I appreciate that, would you rather we dropped the case now?"

For a moment O'Harris almost said yes. He was tired of the anxiety Clara's digging had brought, not to mention the old memories that had resurfaced. Yet he needed a solution, it would unhinge him if he did not know the truth.

"I'll dig up a dozen garages, even this very house if you think it will help."

"Just one garage will do," Clara smiled. "May we discuss servants now? Oh, by the way..."

Clara took the new threatening note she had received from her handbag and showed it to the captain. He studied it carefully.

"Dirty-fingered fellow."

"You think it is a man?"

O'Harris glanced up, uncertain what he had thought.

"I don't know, suppose it just seemed to spring to mind."

"Whatever the case, someone is still trying to scare me off. Male or female, they shall not succeed."

"Have you shown the police?"

"Whatever for?"

O'Harris almost laughed at the genuinely perplexed look Clara gave him.

"They might be interested, don't you think?"

"They showed absolutely no interest in my stalker from the case involving Mrs Greengage."

O'Harris' amusement turned serious.

"How often has this sort of thing happened?"

"Oh, the stalker was nothing, actually he was only trying to pluck up the courage to return to his mother who thought he was dead. He wanted me to intercede. This is quite different," Clara gave him a stern look. "I am not intimidated by it."

"That is plain enough."

"Good, then you shan't now start lecturing me about being careful and watching what I am about?"

O'Harris bit his tongue, he had been about to say just that. In fact, he was going to go as far as to offer his services as Clara's escort and guardian, but her intuitiveness pulled him up short.

"I would never dream of it."

He distracted them both by mixing up a gin and lemon cocktail and escorting Clara to a chair near the large windows where they could watch the rain tumbling down outside.

"So, back to servants?" He asked, "You have the list I made?"

"Yes, not as many as I expected though."

"My uncle and aunt decided to reduce the number of servants in the house around 1900. You have learned enough about old Flo to understand how conscious she was of social change and the needs of others. She thought it very bad for the house to have so many extraneous servants, so she made some cuts."

"Any resentment from it? After all, she was putting people out of work."

"Aunt Flo had more sense than that. She had two girls leave and never replaced them, and she retired some of the older staff off with a pension. I think someone left to tend to their sick mother and she found employment elsewhere for a few others. It was really quite remarkable."

Clara glanced at the list of servants O'Harris had written out for her on their previous meeting when the dead mouse had been first course on the menu.

"So, by 1913 there was a butler, a cook, a housekeeper and a maid working as indoor staff."

"And a woman came in occasionally to clean. She was a widow and needed the extra money. I think she moved to Scotland eventually to be with a sister. I know she is not in Brighton anymore."

Clara added a note to the list with the words 'extra cleaning help,' to refresh her memory later.

"Now your uncle and aunt kept more outside staff."

"Always took more outside staff to run the place than indoor."

"So, there were five gardeners and one head gardener, Mr Riggs?"

"Yes."

"And a gamekeeper?"

"He had his own cottage on the estate. He was in his seventies and didn't really do a lot except wander the forest down the end of the grounds once in a while. Uncle Goddard gave up shooting pheasants years before. He only kept him on as a favour."

"There was a stableman and a stable boy."

"They only kept two horses and a pony. The stable boy doubled up as a garage attendant and kept the cars clean."

"And a chauffeur?"

"Former coach driver. Goddard sent him off to train up on car engines and he was more mechanic than chauffeur. He kept all the cars in pristine order."

"That leaves a land manager."

"He supervised any work on the grounds beyond the skills of the gardeners. He is gone too. I think he died in 1910. He was another old retainer and had really worked beyond when he should."

"Out of these people, then, only three remain here today. The cook, the housekeeper and Mr Riggs. What became of the rest?"

O'Harris flopped back in his chair and swirled the alcohol in his glass.

"Let's see. Can't remember the maid, the one that came after Millie I mean. I don't believe she was local, anyway I had hardly anything to do with her and she left after a year or so to get married."

"Did she know Millie?"

"I couldn't say, but she came here after... well, just after."

Clara nodded.

"What about the butler?"

"Mr Barnstaple was conscripted in 1917, was accidentally gassed by his own side six months later and invalided back to Britain early 1918.

I saw him in the hospital once when I was on leave. He went down with influenza and died of pneumonia later that year."

Clara grimaced as she ticked the name off the list with the notation, 'deceased.'

"What of the gardeners?"

"Three of the younger ones joined up with the first swell of patriotism in 1914, the fourth joined in 1915 after taking insults from the local lads. The under-gardener was conscripted and that left Mr Riggs who I believe was spared service because he was awaiting an operation on a hernia. By the time he was fighting fit, so to speak, the war was over, and the five other gardeners were dead."

"All of them?"

O'Harris lifted up his hand and started tallying off the gardeners one finger at a time.

"Gas, shrapnel, machine-gun, blood poisoning and the under-gardener drowned when the ship bringing him home sank."

"That is rather morbid," Clara said, sickened by the news.

"It gets worse. The stableman went over with our horses. He took Goddard's Hunter called Stanley. Stanley was taken into the cavalry and was lost at the Somme. The stableman was so distraught when he heard Stanley was gone, he deserted and when they caught him, they shot him. Stanley, as it turns out, hadn't died as they all thought. He turned up six days later. Crossed No Man's Land by himself and wandered back to his stables. He came home in 1918 and is out in the paddock as we speak."

Clara was too stunned to know what to say.

"As for the stable boy, he was another early joiner and I think he fell at Ypres. The chauffeur went into the engineering corps because of his talent with engines and was eventually posted to keep those new tanks running. He actually survived, but he fell in love with a French girl and never came home."

"Aside from your chauffeur, that is a very dismal catalogue of misfortune," Clara stared at the list and the notations beside each name. "I hardly know what to say."

"That is war, Clara," O'Harris shrugged. "Care for another drink?"

Clara wouldn't normally but the stories of the lost family servants had upset her, and she handed over her glass absent-mindedly.

"That leaves only three suspects for writing those notes," she said when O'Harris returned with her cocktail.

"What will you do?"

"I need to talk with them, one at a time and see if I can root out who is behind this."

"I'm certain I can arrange that. Do you want it done now?"

Clara was staring at her list.

"Yes," she said numbly. "No time like the present."

Clara had hoped to talk to the cook first, after all she was the one who would feel the full burden of the dead mouse on the serving platter, but she had failed to account for the natural hierarchy that develops among domestic servants. The housekeeper was top of the chain within the household and so she insisted on seeing Clara first. Even O'Harris could not refuse. He gave a wistful shrug and took a chair in the corner of the room where he was almost out of sight.

"Hello Mrs?"

"Abergavanney," The housekeeper declared.

"Mrs Abergavanney, are you aware why we are meeting?"

"It's about that matter with the mouse," the housekeeper screwed her lips up as though she had tasted something bitter. "It is a disgraceful matter and I have had words with cook."

"I am sure, but I would like to find the perpetrator of this practical joke."

"Well don't look at me!" Mrs Abergavanney almost spat out the words, "I have been here 29 years, and never have I caused so much as a moment's discomfort to the occupants. I would not go around planting dead mice in the dinner!"

"I never thought you would," Clara promised, feeling a wave of sympathy for the cook. "I just wondered if you might know who did?"

The pout seemed to become even harder on Mrs Abergavanney's lips.

"I was upstairs at the time. I was having my own lunch in my room. A bowl of plain soup with a crust of bread and a cup of tea. It is quite permitted, ask Captain O'Harris. Mrs O'Harris felt it a mark of respect for my loyalty and time at the house to give me an hour for lunch which I was allowed to take in my room away from the rest of the household."

The speech came out so fast, Clara hardly had time to take it all in.

"I would never imply you would do something improper."

"Nor should you! I know my place. Indeed, I do!"

"You knew nothing about the mouse?"

"Not until that half-wit Maud came bumbling up the stairs yelling it out all about the house. In my day girls knew a bit of decorum, but these days they bawl everything as though they are in the fish market," Mrs Abergavanney was almost trembling with outrage at the scene Maud had made. "I came straight down of course and took one look at the dead thing and asked cook how it had got there, and she of course said she did not know. Well, I was quite put out seeing as I run a clean house, Miss Fitzgerald, and no mouse has dared walk through these doors since before you were born."

Clara quite believed it.

"Thank you, Mrs Abergavanney."

Chapter Twenty

The next to appear was the cook. O'Harris introduced her as Mrs Crimps, who had been with the family at least since 1890.

"1891," Mrs Crimps promptly replied. "Though I weren't cook then, I worked under Mrs Duncan. Those were the days when a cook had more than a maid to help her in the kitchen."

Clara was unclear whether that was an observation or a rebuff of the captain.

"I'm terribly sorry about the mouse," Mrs Crimps' face fell. "Nothing like this has ever happened before. I don't know how it got there."

"You didn't see anyone tamper with the platter?" Clara asked pointedly.

"No... oh but you are thinking I did it? I admit I was the one made up the platter, but I would never risk my position with such a foolish stunt. I've been here too long for games like that, besides, at my age the thought of being out of work is worse than anything else."

Clara had to admit it seemed an unlikely thing for the cook to do, but nothing could be ruled out.

"Let's piece this together a bit better. When did you make the platter?"

"About half an hour before I served it. I wasn't aware we were to have company you see, before then I mean."

"I presume you left it somewhere?"

"In the pantry, where it was cool, but not too cool. Chilled pâté is very poor, it needs to be warm slightly, just enough to bring out the flavour."

"And you saw no one around it?"

"Who would there be but me and Maud? Maud can vouch that I never touched the platter after I covered and put it in the pantry and she never touched it until I said to bring it in to you and I was facing her so I could have seen her tamper with it, and she ain't that kind of girl!"

Mrs Crimps fidgeted anxiously, her tone turning defensive.

"It really is a limited suspect pool," Clara said apologetically, though with a glint in her eye. "Perhaps I could see the pantry?"

Mrs Crimps was flustered as she led Clara and Captain O'Harris into her kitchen. It wasn't right the master of the house coming in and she didn't like the idea of her domain being poked around in by some miss who called herself a detective. She grumbled under her breath as she showed them the pantry.

"Here it is, been here ever since I come," she said rather sharply.

Clara ignored her temper and glanced at the pantry. It offered no inspiration. It was well-lined and clean, a mouse trap sat on the floor but from the condition of the small lump of bread that rested on it as bait there had been no mice present in a long time.

"Where does this door lead to?" Clara pointed to a white door beside the pantry entrance.

"To another passage that has the door to the garden at the bottom."

"Is that unlocked?"

"During the day it is, so Mr Riggs can come in and have a cup of tea."

"Mr Riggs comes into the kitchen?"

"By no means! He works in that filthy garden and his boots are always thick with mud. He has a chair in the passage," Mrs Crimps opened the door and pointed out an old wooden kitchen chair against the far wall. A blast of cold air blew in from the passage and Clara felt infinitely sorry for Mr Riggs who was banished from even drinking his tea in the warmth of the kitchen.

"Were you in the kitchen all that day Mrs Crimps?"

Mrs Crimps started to nod, then shook her head.

"What a question! I think I was, but then how should I know? I nip out all the time for this and that, I had to fetch some parsley for garnish on the sandwiches, I remember that. I keep a pot in the greenhouse, but I was here the rest of the time. Probably."

"I am trying to establish Mrs Crimps if anyone could have entered the kitchen without you knowing?"

"Hardly likely, and who anyway?"

"Mr Riggs?"

The cook gave Clara a firm glare.

"He would not dare, besides this floor is spotless and if he walked in with those enormous boots of his I would have seen the mud."

"Point taken," Clara smiled at the woman trying to defuse her temper. "I should add that in no way am I concerned about your cooking. Indeed, I would partake of lunch any time it was prepared by yourself. The sandwiches were first class."

The flattery worked. Mrs Crimps simmered a moment then relaxed.

"I try my best."

"And you have been here since 1891? You must have seen some changes to the place?" Clara pulled out a stool from under the kitchen table and perched on it, she motioned behind her back for O'Harris to do the same.

Mrs Crimps was calming down now it seemed that Clara had forgotten about the mouse and just wanted to talk. Mrs Crimps supposed it was in the nature of a detective to be nosy.

"I have seen some changes, yes. It was all very different when I first come. There must have been a dozen servants in the house then and a whole army of them outside. I don't exactly miss those days, but the bustle was nice and there was always something going on. Everyone had their story to tell and the maids, oh, they were always up to some mischief. Poor Mrs O'Harris used to get quite despondent at the rate she went through them."

"A lot came and went then?"

"It was the way it was," Mrs Crimps risked the improperness of pulling out her own stool, her joints grew sore in the winter these days and she appreciated sitting down. "Few of them were like me and chose being in service for life. They would be here maybe a few months, sometimes a year or two, then they were married and gone, or..."

"Or, Mrs Crimps?"

The cook blushed a little.

"Back in the days when it was a big household there was a footman here, Gerry the Terror we called him. He was all hands and none of the girls were safe. Oh, he was harmless enough, but if you let him charm you, you could end up in a lot of trouble, as some of the girls discovered."

Clara nodded understandingly. She wished she could signal to O'Harris to leave the room, the questions she wanted to ask next would likely draw a reaction from Mrs Crimps she would want to hide from him.

"Dear captain, I do believe I left my handkerchief in my purse in the drawing room, would you fetch it for me?" Clara finally gave up being subtle.

"I'll send Maud," Mrs Crimps offered quickly.

Clara pinned O'Harris with her firmest stare, hoping to get her point across. It seemed he understood.

"No need Mrs Crimps, I know where it is. I shan't be a moment," the captain stood up.

"No rush," Clara emphasised as he left.

She let the interruption cool down for a moment, making a vague comment about the shine Mrs Crimps had achieve on her copper jelly moulds, then she went back on the attack.

"Now you mention it I do recall a story concerning that footman."

"Really?"

"Well, I believe so. My maid told me it when I mentioned the O'Harris name, she is a dreadful gossip you know."

"Quite, such a nuisance."

"Why she said that there was a girl here who got herself into trouble and fell down the stairs. It was a dreadful accident. Nellie, I think she was called."

"Millie," Mrs Crimps corrected automatically. "But that was after Gerry had left."

"Oh?"

"Yes, I have no idea who the unfortunate girl was involved with, but the outcome was as you said, except several of us here at the time considered it suicide."

"That is quite shocking."

"It happens," Mrs Crimps shook her head. "But she was a wayward girl with an eye for the boys. Indeed, I saw her cast her eye on the good captain, but he had more sense than that."

Clara made no comment.

"She was carrying on with a few of the lads from town, I lost track of them after a while. They were always popping round and bothering us until Mrs Abergavanney had to have words with her. Oh, she put on her parts and threatened to quit, but that didn't help her at all. Mrs Abergavanney said she would help her pack her bag."

"Sounds like she was not terribly popular?"

Mrs Crimps put her head on one side as though she was considering the suggestion.

"She wasn't unpopular. You just couldn't get close to her. She had no friends here, not really. I think she fell in well with some of the gardeners and the stable boy had an eye for her, but that wasn't friendship as such."

"Still her accident must have been a shock."

"Oh yes, I heard her thumping down the stairs myself! What a racket. Poor Mr O'Harris was beside himself. Mrs Abergavanney hardly blinked an eye, but then *she* wouldn't."

"Was anyone, aside from Mr O'Harris upset?" Clara asked in mock surprise.

"Not really. I suppose we were all a little shocked. I had to tell the men outdoors, of course. The gardeners were then coming in for a cup of tea, one lad went pale, but he was a soft soul, so I don't think it were because he was particularly fond of her, just that anything like that made him queasy. The stable boy refused his supper that night, come to think of it."

Clara let her mind absorb the information, but it was too vague and made such little sense. If Millie was the motive for Goddard O'Harris' death Mrs Crimps' story did not point to any of the servants, though it did rather suggest Florence might have had cause to be jealous. Was Goddard so upset simply because of the shock or because Captain O'Harris was not the only one to be smitten by Millie's charms?

"Thank you, Mrs Crimps, I do apologise for holding you up."

"That is perfectly all right my dear. Are you staying for lunch?"

"I have yet to be invited."

"Let me suggest I do it on his behalf," Mrs Crimps surprised Clara by winking at her. "I really want you to try my homemade potted shrimp, it is rather wonderful."

"I should be delighted," Clara made her excuses and went to find O'Harris and inform him he was stuck with her for another hour at least.

The rain had eased up by the time Clara set out on her way home. Captain O'Harris tried to insist on taking her in his car but Clara simply refused. The day was turning out fine and the walk would do her good after the heavy lunch Mrs Crimps had served. She had appeared to want to impress Clara with her culinary skills and had presented a feast of various dishes to be sampled. Besides Clara had a great deal of thinking to do and that was best done alone and while walking.

She wandered down the grand drive noting the spring flowers emerging in patches of colour around the trees and the bent over stems of the previous month's daffodils. A figure was working in the distance, hoeing a flower bed. She eased her stride as she recognised Mr Riggs.

"Good afternoon!" She called jovially.

Mr Riggs looked up, if she had hoped for a guilty expression, she did not get it. He merely took off his cap and nodded to her.

"This is fine weather, is it not Mr Riggs?" Clara smiled, "And your flowers look superb, what a pity I was not here when the Daffs were in bloom."

"Ah, they've had their day now. I've folded 'em over and tied up their stems so they will rot back and be ready for next year."

"That is the thing about gardens, always something to do, always something new happening. They are quite therapeutic, are they not?"

"Ay, I hear as much," Mr Riggs toyed with his cap, seemingly anxious to get on with his hoeing.

"I have had such a morning talking to Mrs Crimps, and she has fed me so much! I dare say she was trying to make up for the last time I had lunch here," Clara gave a light laugh.

"Really miss?" Riggs asked with a singular lack of curiosity.

"Anyway, I think Mrs Crimps was rather enjoying telling me about how things were here in the past. She was telling me about the footman, erm, Gerry, yes that was it."

"I remember Gerry," Mr Riggs nodded. "Had a way with the ladies."

"As she explained, but I did get muddled, I had it in my head he was something to do with a maid called Millie who fell down the stairs here, but it was my mistake. Unless there were two Millies?"

"No, only the one. But that was years ago."

"Yes, quite, and I didn't like to say too much as I thought it might upset the captain. No one likes to think of someone throwing themselves down their staircase."

Mr Riggs eyes widened for a moment.

"I always thought she tripped."

Clara tried to assess his expression, but he seemed genuinely surprised.

"Perhaps I heard that wrong too. Oh dear, it has been such a day," Clara made a pretence of adjusting her hat. "I mustn't delay you Mr Riggs, what are you planting in there?"

"French marigolds," Mr Riggs shrugged.

"I shall look forward to seeing them. Good afternoon," Clara waved goodbye and left the bewildered gardener standing watching her, his hoe idle in his hand.

Chapter Twenty-One

"Let me get this straight, now you think none of them did it?" Tommy peered at Clara over the top of his paper.

"I didn't say that. What I mean, what I think I mean, is that none of them seem to have a motive."

"That is how this case has been all along. You should call it the Mystery of the Motiveless Murder."

"Nothing is motiveless," Clara took off her heels and rubbed her feet, she noticed miserably there was a new ladder in her stockings. "Bother."

"The case is back to suspect No. 1 yet again," Tommy put aside his paper. "Florence O'Harris."

"That worries me, I mean she is the obvious choice, but is she too obvious?"

"Could it be, Clara Fitzgerald, you are stumped?"

Clara gave him a disparaging look.

"Not stumped, just uncertain how this all fits together. But the builders are coming tomorrow to dismantle the front of the O'Harris garage and if we can get at the footings, we may just find a body."

"Bodies preserve well in concrete," Tommy said idly.

"I sometimes wonder how you know these things."

"It is all to do with the oxygen and bacteria not being able to get to the body. I would say that is why fewer criminals do it, you don't exactly dispose of a body."

"You do if the footings are under a house."

"Point taken, but houses get knocked down."

"And gardens dug up and rivers drained, and thick forest cut down, few places are secure for hiding a body."

"Has anyone ever told you two, you are both decidedly morbid?" Annie appeared in the room with two cups of tea.

Clara noted she did not make eye-contact with Tommy the entire time she was in the room and left without another word.

"We have reached a mutual agreement for a brief hiatus on shelling each other," Tommy informed his sister. "Only the shells were rather one-sided and very verbal."

He made a play of rubbing his ears as if they ached.

"When does O'Harris fly?" Clara asked, trying to assuage her anxiety and anger.

"Saturday, all being well. Weather forecast is good for the time of year and promising only light winds."

Clara took a long sip of tea.

"It is such an adventure Clara," Tommy said, beseeching her to understand.

"Of that I am sure," Clara mooted the subject. "I have compiled a new list of suspects, taking into account someone involved in the crime is still alive today and sending those ominous notes. Though we do have to count the possibility they are nothing more than a nuisance from some numbskull."

"Who is on your list?"

Clara groaned.

"Florence O'Harris," she slumped back in the chair. "And her accomplice could be anyone of Mrs Abergavanney, Mrs Crimps, Mr Riggs or Colonel Brandt."

"I suppose the Colonel could send notes, maybe he regrets getting you involved."

"He is in this very deep now Tommy, he told me about Goddard's affair with Susan O'Harris, that raises even more of a dilemma. Do you think Captain O'Harris knows?"

"No, and you can't tell him."

"Can't I?"

"Telling a man his father isn't who he thought he was, is dangerous, especially when that man is about to fly across an ocean. He needs his mind clear."

"Point taken," Clara sighed. "Anyway, I'm not really convinced Mrs Crimps would have tainted her own food, it was too risky, and Mrs Abergavanney appears to have had no reason either, but then that leaves Mr Riggs, and he has no reason as well!"

"There has to be one thread that unravels this all," Tommy assured her.

"I am hoping it is in those cement footings."

"If Goddard O'Harris is lying there, what do you think O'Harris will do?"

Clara honestly didn't know.

"What would you do Tommy? If it was your uncle?"

"Walk away, maybe," Tommy shook his head. "I suppose I would want to know why. It is so hard to say when it isn't yourself involved."

"I wonder if I should call Inspector Park-Coombs?"

"Not until you know something Clara, this could be a wild goose chase."

"Goddard O'Harris has to be buried somewhere."

"Maybe," Tommy drained the last of his tea. "Maybe."

There was no tidy way to demolish the garage and O'Harris had paid for speed not delicacy. After the tiles on the roof and the roof beams were removed the walls were hammered into rubble and crumbled to the ground. The *White Buzzard* stood quietly by, watching the destruction of her home dispassionately.

Clara arrived with Tommy in the late afternoon after receiving a phone call to say the foundations had been uncovered. The first person Clara spotted was Mr Clarence. He tipped his cap to her.

"Thought I should be here, not often one of the things I put up is purposefully knocked down," Mr Clarence looked grim and a tad broken-hearted, Clara supposed it was hard watching your work be destroyed. "I've pointed out the exact spot, the men are getting the pickaxes now."

Captain O'Harris wandered over with Colonel Brandt in tow.

"Sad day," the colonel muttered, "If we find him..."

He blew his nose into a large handkerchief and wandered away again.

"I'm sorry about the garage," Clara said, beside herself at the sadness on O'Harris' face.

"It doesn't matter," he shrugged.

"Do you regret asking me to do this?"

O'Harris suddenly flashed a smile at her.

"Don't be foolish Clara. I knew what I was letting myself in for the moment I asked you. Maybe from the moment I asked you to dinner I had it at the back of my mind I would get you to unravel this mystery. This is painful, but it doesn't mean it shouldn't be done," he suddenly looked at Tommy. "Hey, old chum, how are the legs?"

"A bother," Tommy said glumly.

"There is a doctor who thinks he could help him, but Tommy is being as stubborn as ever and refusing to see him," Clara added.

"Now, old man, that is a bit childish," O'Harris admonished.

Tommy gave a grimace.

"Doctors are all for poking and prodding."

"Not this one," persisted Clara, "Oh if only you would try!"

Tommy looked sullen and O'Harris decided it was best not to encourage an argument.

"I imagine you have heard about my flight on Saturday?" He didn't quite realise the antagonism his new train of conversation would bring.

"Yes, I am aware," Clara answered.

"Will you be on the pier watching?"

She hesitated a moment, her eyes sliding to Tommy.

"I might."

"I would love to see you waving me off, give me a bit of extra courage, you know."

Clara suddenly felt a tide of unhappiness grab her. It had done so before when O'Harris had talked about his flight, but never so powerfully as in that moment. She wanted to tell him to call the thing off, enjoy being Captain O'Harris and living in a fine house, but she knew he would not. Even her friendship could not dissuade him, she saw that in his eyes. Instead, she said what she knew he wanted to hear.

"I shall stand there and wave. I'll wave you both off."

"Good, it will mean a lot," O'Harris grinned at her just as a cry went up.

A builder was waving a chunk of concrete he had just dislodged, and everyone was hurrying over. Owen Clarence pushed forward and took the chunk of grey material. He ran his fingers over the rough edge.

"Something definitely went in, and it trapped some air with it. This edge here is smooth as though there were a gap beneath it."

The workers with the pickaxes were hammering the concrete even faster now they knew they were on the right track. Another lump of concrete broke off and was tossed aside.

"I can make out an 'ole!" One of the men claimed.

Clarence limped over to the scene and peered into the hole.

"Definitely something down there, but it ain't big," he gave a deferential look to O'Harris.

The captain looked pale and grim, his mouth was set in a stiff line and all his usual enthusiasm seemed to have drained from him. Clara felt horrible for what she was causing, she wanted to reach out and touch him. Another piece of concrete was chucked to the side.

"It looks like a cavity, here this piece has got something stuck to it," a worker handed Mr Clarence a shallow shard of grey concrete that had what appeared to be paper stuck on the back.

"What is that?" Clara moved forward for a better look.

"Some sort of printed card, I would say," Clarence gave it to her.

The concrete had clearly stuck to something and when it was now removed the top layer of what it had cemented itself to had come with it. The card was green with a gold edge and there was the faintest impression of letters in a swirling hand. Clara traced them with her finger, trying to reverse them in her head without success.

"I see a box!" Clarence was doing his best to peer into the cavity that had formed, "Chip away the concrete about it and let's see if we can bring it up."

The men set-to with their pickaxes, Clara took a pace back as small, pebble-sized lumps of cement flew into the air.

"Let's take a look," Tommy took the block of concrete off her.

"It seems to have been the lid of a box," Clara said baffled.

"What are these letters? A *b* or a *t*, really quite unclear."

"I think it is a maker's name, but the lettering is very stylised."

"Why would anyone dump a box in a pool of concrete?"

Captain O'Harris was looking at them clearly wondering the same, some of his colour had returned, it seemed they weren't about to find a body.

"Here it comes!" Clarence called.

A workman had managed to get his pick under the lump of concrete containing the box and was levering it up while his colleague reached in and looped his hand underneath. Between the two of them, and with Clarence issuing instructions every moment, they hauled out the box in its casement of concrete.

Clara was first to the find, bending down and brushing off loose grey dust, ignoring the mess it was making of her gloves. Part of the lid had been ripped off by the layer of concrete above it, leaving a thin, blank sheet of cardboard over the box. It was dark green too and must once have been quite thick considering the depth remaining. It was a smart box, no doubt about that.

"Is it jewellery?" A workman asked.

Clara thought not, it wasn't that sort of box. Captain O'Harris had joined her, and Tommy was peering over her shoulder. She tried to lift the lid.

"It's stuck down, perhaps some cement leaked in," she ran her finger down the edge, but the seal was strong. "Tommy, have you your pocketknife?"

Tommy handed over a blade he had had since he was a boy and watched enviously as Clara slotted it into the thin gap between the lid and the box and began working it along. It was like the uncovering of an ancient tomb or treasure and more than one soul was jealous that Clara had seized the initiative first.

"Here, let me try," said Owen Clarence, but Clara ignored him.

The concrete was gradually crumbling as she gently sawed the knife, it was only a very fine layer after all and at points she felt the cardboard of the box rip and let the blade through. She could sense the impatience in the crowd around her as she cut round the last side. The lid was finally free. For a moment she did nothing, after such a long time one could only wonder what horrors lay in the box and had caused its last owner to dispose of it so. It had never meant to be found, that was for sure. Feeling strangely reverential over the box and its contents Clara raised the lid.

"Why it's just a load of old cigars," someone groaned.

Chapter Twenty-Two

Captain O'Harris quickly knelt by Clara. The cigars at the edges of the box had been covered with the seeping cement, but the ones in the middle were as intact as the day they had been made. O'Harris took one.

"These are my father's favourite cigars," he said looking at the gold and green wrapper around the one in his hand.

Clara caught herself before asking whether he meant Oscar or Goddard. He didn't know about his mother's affair, she was sure, and now was not the time to expose it.

"These are your father's cigars?" She asked instead.

"Yes, well, actually this looks like his last box that he bequeathed to Uncle Goddard. They were expensive and he had hardly touched this lot and he knew Aunt Flo never allowed Goddard to spend as much as these cost on cigars, she considered it a frivolous waste. I always thought it quite touching he left his last box to his brother. He even made a point, when he knew he was dying, to not touch these ones so Goddard would have almost a full box. Considering the difficulties they had, it was quite moving."

Clara was eyeing the box and thinking, slowly ideas were forming in her mind.

"'ere, do we get a cigar for unearthing 'em?"

Clara didn't even glance up. She took the cigar back from O'Harris and put it in the box.

"No, these are evidence."

"Evidence?" The workman who had asked pouted, "Evidence of what?"

"Murder, maybe."

"It ain't a body!"

There was some disgruntled grumbling in the crowd.

"That's enough you lot," Captain O'Harris took charge. "You were employed to demolish a garage and I shall pay you well for that, but you weren't here for a treasure hunt and can't expect a share of what we found. Besides those cigars have been encased in concrete for over ten years."

"Still would have liked to try one," someone muttered.

"Get your minds off old cigars and back onto putting my garage back together," O'Harris shepherded the men back to work and wandered away from Clara.

Quietly she passed the box to Tommy.

"I have an awful hunch Tommy," she said.

"Why throw a box of expensive cigars into concrete foundations? Yes, I was thinking it looks rather suspicious too."

"If it was gas it had to get into Goddard somehow," Clara caught her brother's eye. "He went out to smoke a cigar the night he died."

"It would have been quick," Tommy nodded. "Risky though, if he smoked indoors, he could have taken out Florence as well."

"He never smoked indoors. Florence never allowed it. Besides, the murderer might not have cared. Will you ask the Colonel to help you escort these to the police station and ask for them to be tested?"

"I will, but what will you do?"

"I want to know more about Oscar O'Harris, about his real relationship with Goddard, especially after Susan O'Harris' confession."

"All right, but tread softly."

"When do I not?" Clara pretended to be offended, "And don't let those cigars out of your sight until they are in the hands of a police chemist. The Colonel is still technically a suspect after all."

"If they find what you expect them to find, this will narrow our search."

"Probably."

"I'll get on to it right away," Tommy went to find the colonel while Clara approached O'Harris.

"I've put Tommy in charge of the cigars," she said casually.

"Oh, right," O'Harris looked distracted.

"Are you... disappointed there wasn't a body?"

"I don't know," O'Harris gave a shrug. "Maybe. I thought we might resolve this thing once and for all."

"Look, I could do with a hot cup of tea after all this excitement. What do you say?"

O'Harris at last turned his attention to Clara.

"You're a remarkable girl," he said with a broad grin. "You didn't flinch a hair when that box came up."

Clara felt that many women would have been of a similar stoic nature, it was only a box after all.

"I don't really do flinching, it is unprofessional, but I would like a cup of tea."

"Of course," O'Harris offered his arm and she accepted though it seemed a trifle old-fashioned. "I'll have Mrs Crimps run something up at once."

They progressed to the drawing room and sat near the window to capture the afternoon sun.

"Were you expecting a box?"

"No," Clara answered. "I had really thought we might find a body."

"I'm rather relieved – now I have had time to think it over – that it was just a box. Though it seems strange the cigars were thrown away. Do you suppose Flo did it? Or a servant?"

Clara was not inclined to speculate until the verdict on the cigars was in.

"I don't know, it might have been an accident. Did no one miss the cigars after Goddard's funeral? Such as it was."

"It was a memorial service. I think there is something against having a funeral with no body. Anyway, there was no one really to notice. I don't smoke cigars, so I never would have even thought of them, and you know Flo's thoughts on the subject."

"Yes," Clara gazed out the window noticing Mr Riggs wandering across the garden, a dead rat hanging by its tail from his hand. That was another loose end to tie up. But Mr Riggs would never have had access to Goddard's cigars.

"So those were your father's favourites?" She said to shift the subject in a more promising direction.

"Yes, he was partial to a good cigar. The doctors said they would do his cancer the world of good, but I'm afraid that was not the case. I always bought him a cigar for Christmas. Something different, one he hadn't tried before. I became quite familiar with the inside of a tobacconist's shop, I tell you! When I was a boy, I saved up my pennies but could only buy the cheapest of things. Despite that he always smoked them. He made a big show of taking out the cigar I had bought and lighting it up right after Christmas dinner. I'm sure some of them were foul things!"

"You were close then?"

O'Harris thought for a moment.

"I would say so, well as close as any lad is to his father. He was a good sort, always had time for me. We used to build forts out of the dining room furniture together and he helped me construct elaborate railway tracks for my trains. He was a fun old thing, he liked science, not history like Goddard. History he found dull, but he liked how you could mix two chemicals together and get the most extraordinary reactions. He used to embroil me in his experiments. He had a book on amateur science, and he would find an experiment he fancied and have all the stuff waiting and ready for when I was home from school. We always did the experiments together. And he loved astronomy as well, winter and summer we would climb to the roof of our house and gaze at the constellations."

Clara was sure her heart was pounding and wondered if it showed.

"Your father was a chemist then?"

"Oh, nothing as formal as that, he just liked to dabble. He tried photography as well, that fascinated him, and the natural world. He had a small egg collection which he was very precious about, though he refused to take more than one egg from a nest as he didn't want to reduce the number of birds. He had a tame magpie, actually, well for a year or so, then I think it flew away."

"He sounds a very interesting man. I'm surprised he didn't get on better with Goddard."

"But he did, what gave you the idea he didn't?"

"Well, the talk of him arguing with Goddard and then hardly visiting."

"That?" O'Harris shook his head, "That was a one-off nonsense over money, and it wasn't father who refused to come here, it was mother. Yes, mother got this bee in her bonnet that she wasn't welcome in the house and, especially after I was born, she apparently refused to come here, except on the odd occasion. Which is quite a shame for I don't think Flo was really that objectionable towards her and father did miss Goddard."

"Really?"

"You couldn't call them close, not like ordinary siblings because there was such an age gap. But he respected Goddard, always looked up to him and thought the world of him. It struck me, as I got older, that he hero-worshipped my uncle, but I suppose that was natural considering Goddard had been in the military and had done such marvellous things, while my poor father remained at home and drifted about. Aside from marrying my mother he really failed to do anything worthwhile." O'Harris laughed.

"And then he sadly got ill," Clara was rapidly piecing things together; the heroic elder brother, the idolising younger brother, the marriage that had tipped the balance and the son that had resulted from it.

O'Harris went quieter as talk turned to his father's demise.

"I sometimes wonder if there is a streak of bad health in the O'Harris line," he pressed the tips of his fingers together and tapped them against his lips. "My mother and father both died before their time. Mother was swept away by some sort of internal complaint. The doctor was rather obtuse about the whole matter. Women's business I took it to mean. She died in a lot of pain and that troubled me greatly. Dying doesn't bother me, but pain does. I would have done anything to spare her that."

"Did you see her much when she was dying?" Clara wondered if Susan O'Harris had felt like confessing all to her son too.

"Not really, I was then at school, for what good it did me. I really hated all that, I never could understand how my professors could make the same science my father had made so exciting, so utterly boring. I saw mother maybe twice before the end. It was never made clear to me how sick she really was."

"No doubt she wanted to protect you," Clara said softly, knowing she was touching raw wounds and that she would have to go deeper to clarify her own thoughts.

"Maybe. Father's death was different. It took longer, I mean he was ill for a long-time and there was no hiding it. He looked decrepit, honestly it was shocking. He tried to keep jolly but every time I came home, I saw more marks of pain on his face."

"Cancer is awful."

"Do you have living parents Clara?" O'Harris asked.

She shook her head.

"I lost them both in a bombardment. They were unlucky, they were visiting London when a Zeppelin came over and dropped bombs."

"That is awful," O'Harris reached for her hand and squeezed it lightly. "I don't know if that is worse, not seeing it coming, or watching a person you love wither away."

"Still, at least he was able to write a will and even leave bequests. That was thoughtful."

"I know, which is why it actually pains me to think of his cigars discarded like that," O'Harris was baffled by the discovery. "Why would anyone throw them away?"

Clara didn't care to voice her theories just then. She carefully removed her hand from his.

"People behave oddly when they are grieving."

"It had to be Aunt Flo, she was the only one who could have had access to them," O'Harris shook his head. "It almost seems spiteful."

"I think she took your uncle's death quite hard."

"Do you?"

Clara was pained by the look of hope on his face.

"But, of course, I am still going around in circles. If we had found..." She stilled her tongue.

"If we had found a body, things would have been different, I know," O'Harris finished for her. "As it is Uncle Goddard is missing somewhere still."

Clara leaned back in her chair, watching Riggs returning from his gardening duties. She sank into deep thought, despite what she said to O'Harris things were coming together. The cigars were more than just another clue and the motive for disposing of them could be the key to the murderer. Hadn't Florence encouraged the building work to continue so that the foundations would be poured and thus she had a hiding place for them? Or was it just coincidence? She thought of motive again, did Florence have one? There was her husband's affair with Susan O'Harris, but did she know about it and, anyway, that was years before his death. If she did plot his demise, it was a long time coming, but there was one avenue Clara had almost ignored.

"Do you recall an Edward Highgrove?" She asked casually enough, "He was a cousin of your aunt's, I think."

O'Harris didn't answer at once, considering the question thoughtfully.

"He could have been a cousin, but the name doesn't ring a bell. Why do you ask?"

"His name cropped up," Clara admitted. "And I had the impression she was rather fond of him, even thought about marrying him. But he went off with another girl and then Florence married Goddard O'Harris."

"Poor Flo," O'Harris whistled through his teeth. "What rotten luck. She never talked of an Edward."

"It was just one of those loose ends that came up," Clara felt Edward was another dead end, too much time had again passed for him to be a motive for murder.

"I don't know the Highgrove side of the family well," O'Harris added. "They have always been a solemn lot and really want little to do with the O'Harris side of things. They don't like the fact that there is a touch of Irish blood in the line."

"Ah," Clara nodded knowingly.

They were silent a moment more, then Clara felt she could sit still no longer; she was itching to get to the police station and see what news they had.

"I must get on captain."

"Oh, all right," O'Harris smiled sadly. "Look, Clara, can I ask one more thing."

"Yes, go ahead."

"It's an awkward imposition, I know, but I would really like to have an answer to this mystery before I fly on Saturday. It seems important, somehow, that I know before then."

Clara felt that familiar chill run down her spine.

"I can't promise anything."

"I know, but… if you could just tell me, one way or the other, whether you think my Aunt Flo killed my uncle before Saturday, well, I could fly out with one less worry on my mind. Your opinion counts for a lot, Clara, whatever you say, I'll believe you."

Clara didn't like the responsibility being thrust upon her, she felt as though she was being asked to decide a man's fate.

"I'll do my best," she said, really not wanting to promise anything.

"Good. I really need to know Clara. Before Saturday, I really need to know."

Chapter Twenty-Three

Inspector Park-Coombs gave her a curious smile.

"You've really had the lab boys in a tizzy," he laughed. "In comes Tommy with a box of half-rotten cigars demanding they are tested at once, murder weapons he is calling them. Says they are filled with components to make arsine gas and that they could have killed Goddard O'Harris. Well, you can imagine the disbelief on everyone's faces."

They were heading to the laboratory at the back of the ground floor of the police station, and Inspector Park-Coombs was enjoying his storytelling.

"Of course, you can't ignore such a thing, not really. Not when it has been sent by Clara Fitzgerald herself," the inspector gave her a wink. "The box was duly sent to the lab boys who laughed even harder than the rest of us when they were told the story."

They reached a brown door marked *private*. The inspector turned the handle and pushed it open. Just beyond was a scene Clara recalled from her days at school. Not that *girls* in her school had been allowed to dabble in chemistry, but they took their sewing class in the laboratory where the boys were allowed to conduct experiments. The room at the police station had the same smell of spilled chemicals and cleaning fluids and the same array of heavy brown tables, glass vials, tubes, and half-puzzled looking boys in white lab coats.

Clara stepped inside. Straight ahead of her she spotted the open box of cigars.

"Well?" She asked the room at large, several stunned faces turned towards her.

Inspector Park-Coombs strolled in behind Clara.

"This is the lady who nearly poisoned you lot," he grinned at the assembled scientists.

There was an instant chorus of protests:

"Should have warned us!"

"Bloody lethal!"

"Could have taken us all out!"

Clara looked at them sternly.

"You were warned," she said bluntly. "You chose not to believe a mere woman."

Silence awkwardly fell.

"I take it the cigars were definitely tainted?"

No one at first answered, the inspector scowled at them.

"Answer the lady!" He snapped.

A man wearing a white lab coat was standing by the main table in the room. He straightened his jacket and approached Clara.

"They were laced with various chemicals which, when they interacted, would produce a small but lethal amount of arsine gas," the scientist motioned to the box. "Would you care for me to demonstrate?"

"That won't be necessary…"

Clara interrupted the inspector.

"Yes, I would like to see for myself."

The inspector grimaced as they were escorted to a glass box set near a window.

"This is a sealed glass chamber," the scientist continued, he took a cigar from the box and placed it inside. "I'll poke a short paper wick into the end of the cigar and light it while the box is open. Then I will seal it tight, and the wick will burn down eventually igniting the cigar."

He proceeded to do as he had said. Hastily dropping the cigar into the container once the wick was lit and closing the box. There was a sucking noise as the rubber seals around the box lid gripped each other.

"It creates a vacuum," the scientist continued. "With enough air left inside to keep the wick burning."

The wick was indeed burning fast and within moments it reached the tip of the cigar which started to glow red.

"Ideally it would have a person drawing on it," the scientist shrugged. "Understandably there were no volunteers."

For a while, the cigar burned mildly and without any obvious result. Then a thin trail of smoke rose up.

"Is that arsine gas?" The inspector asked nervously.

"No, that is ordinary smoke. Arsine gas is colourless and odourless, however, when it comes into contact with a polished piece of glass it will form a black film," the scientist opened a small box and produced just such a piece of glass. "Mingled with that smoke you see is arsine gas. Should I open this box you would note a faint garlic smell, right before you died. That is caused by the arsenical reaction which results in the gas. On our first attempt we were slightly incautious with this experiment, being of the opinion this was a load of nonsense. We neglected to use a wick and the lid was still up when our man Evans caught the faintest of aromas of garlic. We closed the lid quickly and dispersed from the room. Evans collapsed outside the door, and it took several minutes to rouse him."

"You were lucky," Clara nodded.

"Our next experiment we put a mouse in the box with the cigar. It died within a second of the smoke rising from the cigar, so we were certain then we had poisonous gas on our hands. We had to do a few more experiments before we could confirm it was arsine."

Clara tried not to think about the poor mouse as she continued with the questions.

"This could kill a man?"

"Yes, virtually instantly."

"And then the gas would disperse?"

"Yes, arsine, unlike some gases which are heavy and will lie close to the ground, is light and is quickly blown away by the wind. It was probably gone within a minute or two. But it would have lasted long enough to kill."

"I have to hand it to you Clara," Park-Coombs rubbed at his chin. "You've unravelled this mystery for certain. Poisoned cigars, that's a new one."

"The person who made this," Clara watched the smoke twirling in the glass box, "How knowledgeable would they have needed to be?"

She addressed the scientist.

"About chemistry? Well, this is actually quite sophisticated. Not something you could cook up in an afternoon. You would need to have a working knowledge of the chemicals involved and have done previous tests on arsenic to produce arsine gas and then you would have had to experiment with various means of combining the chemicals to achieve the gas when the cigar was lit. I say a person had to be confident with chemistry, even if they weren't a professional."

"You have a suspect in mind Clara?" Park-Coombs asked.

"I do, but I am afraid he is long dead."

The smoke twirled upwards in the box, until abruptly the red glow of the cigar was snuffed out and the grey smoke lingered just beneath the lid of the box.

"It's used up all the oxygen," the scientist explained.

"This was a very clever way of killing someone," Clara was musing but she was also curious as to the other men's thoughts.

"It was incredibly subtle, and the incident could have occurred at any time," confirmed the scientist. "As far as we can tell all the cigars were tainted. Which implies the killer wanted to make certain the first time they were smoked they killed."

"Thank you, you have been most helpful."

The scientist gave a smile that quickly turned into a grimace.

"Next time we are sent something based on a Clara Fitzgerald hunch, we'll be more careful with it."

Clara took that as an acknowledgement of her abilities and felt satisfied with herself as she left the room with the inspector.

"So, who committed the murder?" Park-Coombs asked.

"A dead man. In fact, he was dead before the murder even took place."

The inspector gave her a doubting look.

"Those cigars were given to Goddard O'Harris by his brother Oscar who was fascinated by amateur science and quite good at experiments in chemistry, according to his son. He bequeathed the cigars in his will, knowing his brother would be delighted with them because they were more expensive than anything he smoked."

"But he had poisoned them, why?"

"That is complicated Inspector and not something I would care to broadcast publicly."

"Miss Fitzgerald, I am a police inspector! I shall not say a word."

Clara took a moment to decide.

"All right, Oscar O'Harris was furious with his brother because on his wife's deathbed it was revealed to him that Captain John O'Harris was not his son, but the son of Goddard O'Harris. Susan O'Harris, Oscar's wife, had had a brief affair with her brother-in-law and became pregnant as a result."

"But that was years ago!"

"Yes, but the news was fresh to Oscar and hurtful for a lot of reasons. Oscar could not have children, at least that was what he had thought until the arrival of his son John. Knowing John was really Goddard's son was a real kick in the teeth."

"Or, I suppose, his manhood," the inspector nodded with understanding. "That can make a man bitter."

"How long after the confession he concocted his plan we will never know. Perhaps it was when he knew he was dying from cancer. In any case, at some point he poisoned the cigars and came up with the idea of bequeathing them to his brother."

"They gave the appearance of a thoughtful gift, the last act of an affectionate brother."

"Precisely," Clara paused in her tracks. "Horrible, isn't it?"

"So how did they end up in concrete foundations?"

"I'm still working on that," Clara told him, before she let herself out of the police station.

Back home she slumped into her favourite armchair beside the fire. She felt drained both emotionally and physically. She had never expected this case to result in a happy ending for O'Harris; she had always sensed that the crime was an 'inside job' as Tommy's American detective books put it. It had to have been committed by a member of the family or a close friend and as such the hurt O'Harris would suffer from the solution of it would be immense. The 'Millie the maid theory' was long gone, she had been a complicated diversion but, in the end, it seemed no one cared enough about her to avenge her death, or at least did not suspect Goddard of being the father of her child. Perhaps the servants understood Goddard better than she had first thought. This shy, strange man crippled by conflict yet fascinated by its history, unable to come close to his wife, leaving her unloved and, Clara supposed, their marriage unconsummated. Such a thing is talked of among servants.

Then there was the radiant Susan O'Harris. Had she not been so determined to secure her husband's money no doubt she too would have failed to attract Goddard's attention. But she knew how to use her body, oh she knew. Colonel Brandt might fool himself by saying she was a 'genuine' actress, but there was more than a trace of whore about her from what Clara could see. Goddard was not the first man she had seduced, perhaps neither was he the last. But on this occasion, she was careless – or perhaps she meant to get pregnant, to have a hold over Goddard forever, to have a knife she could stab in her husband's back at any moment. It was just horrid, and slap bang in the middle of it was Captain O'Harris, innocent to his parents' failings, but ultimately the one who would suffer.

Clara groaned softly as the inevitable headache came on. She wished she had never taken on this project, more so she wished she had never grown to like Captain O'Harris.

Tommy wheeled himself into the parlour.

"Well?"

"Arsine gas in every single one of them."

He pushed himself up to the table, a thoughtful frown creasing his face.

"I've been thinking about all this while you were gone. I went through the diaries again. It troubled me Florence might have been involved."

"The cigars were made by someone with skill as a chemist, only Oscar O'Harris had that."

"Yes, but that doesn't mean Florence was not complicit in the matter. I've gone through every word for a clue on this case. I can't say for certain Florence helped poison her husband, but nor can I say she didn't."

"You mean, if she too knew about Goddard's infidelity she might have conspired with Oscar?" Clara's eyes stung and she shut them. "I don't know, she was fond of Goddard."

"But it had to be her that threw away the cigars!"

Clara knew that was logical.

"I'm not convinced though."

"There is one person who might be able to give an insight into this. What about Colonel Brandt?"

Clara wondered if she had the energy to go to Brandt's club that night and fight her way past the butler.

"I take your point. I will go and see the Colonel tomorrow."

"Good, perhaps at last this mystery is behind us."

Clara opened her eyes and stared at her brother. Her older brother who she loved so dearly and was terrified of losing.

"Tommy. Captain O'Harris has asked me to tell him who killed his uncle before he flies on Saturday, he seems to think it is important. I have this awful feeling..." Clara hesitated, would he think she was making more difficulties for him, "I have this feeling he is concluding his life here, drawing a line under it, as though he doesn't expect to come back."

"Don't worry about him, old thing. He has a trusty co-pilot on board," Tommy flashed her a grin and Clara felt her resilience weaken. How could she explain that nagging doubt? It was just a feeling anyway.

"How is Annie?" She partially changed the subject.

"She didn't shout at me today, which is a start. Look, Friday night, O'Harris has asked me to spend the night at his. You know, with the flight taking place the next morning."

"Of course," Clara nodded; it was an obvious arrangement.

"You might not believe this, old thing, but he is actually quite worried himself. I think he is looking to me for a touch of moral support, imagine that?"

Clara smiled at him, she realised he was enjoying being the one someone needed, the one someone relied on. She couldn't snatch that from him.

"Keep him company Tommy and let him know my best wishes and prayers fly with him."

"Didn't think you believed, old thing?"

Tommy was teasing but the joke made Clara pause anyway.

"Even the best of us can falter," she replied with a smirk, but deep down she knew something else was stirring.

Chapter Twenty-Four

Colonel Brandt looked a decade older as he lounged in a rocking chair in the club gardens. There was a glass of whisky in his hand, though it wasn't yet ten o'clock. Clara found him easily enough; he was the only soul around.

"Hello," Brandt glanced up. "Who let you in then?"

"The butler's back was turned. I really couldn't be bothered with him today. The place is empty anyway."

"Yes, only us old men get up this early. I'm nursing the same headache I tried to drown out the night before with alcohol," Brandt waved his glass. "I fear I'm failing."

Clara found a garden chair and drew it next to the colonel. He seemed tired and weary; his hand had a distinct shake to it.

"Are you up for answering some questions?" She asked, "I think this will be the last time I need to bother you."

"You are close to a solution?"

"Yes."

"Go ahead then, ask what you need."

Clara composed herself, she had to be tactful and refrain from stirring up the colonel's suspicions. In that case, she suspected she would have to be devious.

"The cigars."

"Yes."

"They were fine," Clara lied. "They were a dead end. Why anyone ever threw them in that concrete..."

Clara let the sentence hang in the air, as she expected the colonel filled the space.

"Florence always hated cigars. I think she threw them in. I thought that the moment I saw them. Do you know how she hated Oscar for sending that box to Goddard? It was palpable."

"I don't understand."

"Florence was convinced smoking cigars weakened Goddard's heart. The doctor said it was harmless, but Florence was certain. She said the way Goddard coughed after smoking one was awful and, sometimes, he would feel pains in his chest. She confided this in me because she was scared. I never knew why she was so frightened."

"Goddard's doctor had diagnosed him with a weak heart," Clara interposed.

"Really? He never told me," the colonel tutted. "He always was so secretive. No wonder Florence was so worried."

"Did she ever try to stop him smoking?"

"Oh yes, she refused to let him spend money on expensive cigars thinking he would hate the cheaper ones but, well, he didn't. And she made him smoke outside, another one of her tricks to try and persuade him to give up, she knew if she confronted him head on, he would become defensive and start smoking in secret. That would have been even worse. As it was, she could just about control his smoking."

"Oscar's bequest would have stung."

"Immensely, in fact she was furious. She told me so; we were at the stage when she confided in me a lot because she was so worried. She wanted to be rid of the things, but she couldn't think how. She even tried to persuade me to take them. She thought I could somehow conjure up a way to make Goddard give them to me. I refused. It was absurd."

Clara briefly closed her eyes, unnerved by how close Colonel Brandt had come to his own end.

"Colonel," She phrased her next question carefully, "What was Florence's opinion of Oscar O'Harris, or rather, did they get along?"

The colonel considered the question carefully.

"I'm afraid they didn't, get along that is. Florence did not exactly hate Oscar, but she disapproved of him. She thought he was a wastrel and when he married Susan, well…"

"Could she have learned of the affair?"

"I can't say for certain, but Goddard was not a man for confessing his soul to anyone. That he told me was remarkable in itself. She may have suspected, perhaps, but I never saw any sign of it."

"And Oscar, did he respond to Florence's disapproval with his own?"

"He hardly visited in the last few years of his life. When he did it was usually at Christmas. After Susan died, I think he was asked a few times, for family's sake, but he rarely actually went. He wrote to Goddard often enough, that was about their only correspondence. I've been there on a cold Christmas morning when the atmosphere inside the house between Florence and Oscar was as chilly as the breeze blowing outside. Do you know, it almost occurred to me that Oscar sent those cigars to spite Florence! It would be his style. He did all he could to snipe at her and spoil anything she had arranged when he visited."

Clara mused on the different perspectives people could have on the same matter. Captain O'Harris thought his father had sent the cigars out of the kindness of his heart, because of his fondness for his brother, the colonel thought it was because he wanted to spite Florence by playing on her concerns and Clara now knew he had sent them to kill his brother.

"I have to ask one last thing Colonel, and I beg you to be entirely honest with me, for the captain's wellbeing is staked on this."

"You do sound serious Miss Fitzgerald."

Clara could hardly express the terrible dread building inside her as Saturday approached; she was sure the answer she gave Captain O'Harris would had an impact on his flight.

"In your opinion could Florence ever work with Oscar to the detriment of Goddard?"

For an instant, the colonel looked stunned, then he laughed so hard he spilt some of his whisky.

"Bless you, I have needed such a good joke for days," the colonel dabbed tears from his eyes with a handkerchief. "Florence would neither write to Oscar nor speak to him unless she had to. Honestly, the woman despised him. When he died, she came close to refusing to go to the funeral, but Goddard reminded her it would look dreadfully bad, and you know how Florence felt about that. In some ways I think she wished it could have been different, but it never was. As for conspiring together? You might as well suggest the Kaiser work with Lloyd George!"

The colonel smiled as he drained his whisky.

"Oh, Miss Fitzgerald these last few days have been Hell."

"Then it is high time I told you Florence O'Harris did not kill her husband."

Brandt looked at her sharply.

"Truly?"

"Truly, she had motive enough, mind you. An unconsummated marriage, the coldness of her husband, the despair of being betrayed by the first man she loved, her cousin, and marrying Goddard instead. The affair between Susan and Goddard, if she had known, but despite all that I think she genuinely cared for her husband and grieved his loss."

"Yes, yes I do too. But, do you know who did kill him?"

Clara looked away from the colonel staring across the grass and newly flowering pansies.

"Oscar O'Harris killed his brother. The cigars, they were poisoned."

Colonel Brandt sank a little in his chair, some weight appeared to lift off him, but his eyes watered.

"Because of John O'Harris?"

"Yes. He could not forgive his brother for having an affair with his wife and producing the son he could not."

There was another long silence.

"You said the cigars were harmless."

"I know, I didn't want news they were poisoned to taint what you said about Florence's feelings on Goddard's smoking habit."

"You thought I might lie?" Brandt was hurt.

"No. But we can unconsciously adjust the truth when we feel the need. You might have felt the need to protect Florence."

Brandt let out a long sigh.

"Then it is all over, except for locating Goddard's grave. Still no luck?"

"I'm working on it, but at least I have an answer for Captain O'Harris."

The colonel nodded.

"I'm sorry the truth could not bring them back," Clara reached over for his hand, it was cold beneath her fingers. She squeezed it.

"Don't worry about that," the colonel gave her a stoical smile. "Us army souls are made of tough stuff."

"I hope so Colonel Brandt, as I expect you to come for dinner on Saturday night."

The colonel started to stutter, not knowing what to say, but before he could refuse Clara was on her feet and leaving.

"I shall be all on my own on Saturday and I could use a friend. I consider you a friend and as such I shall expect you for dinner. We dine at six."

The colonel was still stammering and stuttering as she left.

Tommy was sitting up the parlour table when she got home. He tossed a letter towards her.

"It came a few moments ago."

Clara picked up the envelope and looked at the scrawled handwriting on the back, Miss Fitzgerald was carved into the paper in large letters.

"Another threat," Clara sighed and disposed of her gloves before she opened the letter. Inside was a slip of thick greasy paper with a familiar message.

"Back off, let the dead rest!"

She showed it to Tommy.

"This gets even more bizarre. The killer is dead, who on earth could be writing this?"

"You are overlooking the fact that Oscar must have had an accomplice. Ghosts can't steal and hide bodies, but someone moved Goddard."

"And this accomplice is still alive."

"It appears so."

"Well, the crime is solved. They have no reason to disturb you further since you won't be poking around any longer."

"On the contrary," Clara put the letter neatly in her handbag, "I still have a body to find."

Tommy glared at her.

"Why? You solved it, why stir up more trouble from whoever it is writing these notes."

"Because Goddard O'Harris is lying somewhere in an unmarked grave. He deserves a Christian burial, and no troublemaker will stop me doing that."

Chapter Twenty-Five

On Friday afternoon Clara escorted Tommy to O'Harris' house. They were warmly welcomed and ushered into the drawing room where O'Harris had a fire burning against the unseasonal chill in the air.

"Thank you for coming Tommy, look Clara, about tomorrow..."

Clara interrupted before he could say more.

"It is Tommy's decision, not mine," she answered calmly enough, though in fact she felt sick to her stomach.

O'Harris gave her a curious look but let the subject drop.

"I'm glad you're here, I thought you might avoid me since I was pushing you to give me an answer on Uncle Goddard's death."

"I would never avoid you," Clara said, offended. "I would not be so cowardly, if I could not give you an answer, I would say so to your face."

"Good!" O'Harris grinned at her. "You are a fine woman, Miss Fitzgerald. I wish I could persuade you to fly."

"The old girl barely would get in your motor car," Tommy added.

O'Harris laughed, though Clara pursed her lips indignantly and glared at her brother.

"Never mind that, next plane along I am calling Clara, how about that?"

"I wish her well," Clara said politely.

"She'll be dogmatic, head-strong and murder to control," Tommy elaborated, enjoying teasing his sister. O'Harris restrained his laughing this time seeing how cross Clara was getting.

"Enough of this talk, have you found me an answer?" He leaned forward in his chair eagerly.

"Steady on, chum, you haven't poured us drinks yet," Tommy gave a feigned hurt look. "I'm parched."

O'Harris chortled again as he jumped up to fetch drinks for everyone. Clara cast a glance at her brother for the first time realising how much he enjoyed the friendship of Captain O'Harris. Well, long may it last, he deserved a spark of happiness in his life.

"Here you go," O'Harris had made them all whisky and tonic. Clara sipped hers noncommittally and then put it aside hoping Tommy would be his usual self and steal it when he thought she wasn't looking.

"An answer, Miss Fitzgerald, an answer. Please tell me you have one," O'Harris no longer looked excited or jovial, his tone was deadly serious.

"I do have an answer for you," Clara began, "and I am relieved to say your Aunt Florence had nothing to do with your uncle's death."

O'Harris almost collapsed into a chair.

"That is better news than you could imagine."

"I hope so, but unfortunately I also have some bad news. I know who killed your uncle and it will not please you."

"If it wasn't Flo how can the answer distress me? No, you have to speak up, I need to know."

Clara had dreaded this moment with every ounce of her being. O'Harris' aunt was not a killer, but his father was, it was hardly a good exchange, far from it. She didn't want to tell him and yet at the same time she had no choice. She could lie, but Clara hated such tricks, especially when it came to judging whether to tell someone something. She never seemed able to make the right decision.

"Please, Clara, whatever it is, however bad, please, I need to know," O'Harris begged her with his eyes. Finally, Clara knew she would have to speak.

"I have pieced together the story, though there are still some parts missing. Goddard O'Harris walked out of his dining room to smoke a cigar and never came back. It was murder all right, and it was the cigar he smoked that killed him. The materials within it were laced with chemicals that would produce arsine gas when ignited."

"But the cigars..."

"They came from your father, yes. I am afraid to say I believe the evidence indicates quite strongly that he poisoned them, to enact revenge on your uncle from beyond the grave."

O'Harris stood abruptly and paced about the room, he turned sharply.

"Why?"

"Many reasons, he had conflicts with his brother over money, over his wife. He disliked Florence, it may even in part have been to spite her. But we must also bear in mind he was very ill and sickness, especially cancer, can twist a person's thinking until it is no longer logical or familiar to them."

"You realise what you are saying?"

"Fully."

O'Harris sat again.

"The cigars, he... but Flo threw them away?"

Clara recognised the desperation, suddenly it would not be so bad for his aunt to be the killer.

"I believe she had no knowledge of the cigars being poisoned. She threw them away because she felt they had caused Goddard's death, but not in the manner it had actually happened. She was terrified her husband would smoke himself to death; that the cigars would finish off his weak heart. When he died it seemed that prediction had come true, and she threw away the cigars in a rage. It was a coincidence, I think, nothing more."

"You've done tests and things?"

"Yes."

"And you know... for sure?"

"The cigars belonged to your father; he bequeathed them to your uncle. The murderer had to have a working knowledge of chemistry. You told me yourself your father did."

"You tricked me that day we talked about my father! You had me tell you about his hobbies so you could pin him for this?" O'Harris' shock had turned to anger, and he looked belligerent.

Tommy watched cautiously as the man clenched and unclenched his fists.

"I'm sorry I tricked you," Clara said gently. "I hardly believed it myself, but you wanted the truth."

O'Harris suddenly went still. He was defeated, he had the truth and it burned worse than the terrible dread of thinking his aunt was a killer.

"You weren't supposed to find out something like this," he said miserably. "Not like this, not like this."

"I'm sorry," Clara could think of nothing else to say. She looked to Tommy for assistance, but he had no wise words to offer either.

"Perhaps it was an accident at the cigar manufacturers. Perhaps they somehow contaminated the tobacco?" O'Harris said desperately.

Clara made no reply, it was blatantly apparent that was not the case.

"My father was a good man," O'Harris insisted.

"It would have been the cancer old man," Tommy offered a shred of consolation. "It would have marred his thinking."

"I told you there was a streak of ill-health in my family," O'Harris almost accused Clara. "I told you, perhaps insanity too."

"Perhaps," Clara felt sick to her stomach. This was the man who was to get in a plane tomorrow with her brother and fly across an ocean. Considering the state he was in, how could she trust him with Tommy's life? She wished she had said she didn't know, why had she been so determined to tell the truth?

O'Harris was up again and pacing.

"Who hid the body then, huh?"

"I don't know as yet, but whoever it was, is most likely the same person who keeps writing threatening notes to me."

O'Harris paced, but he was slowing.

"You've had more?"

"One more," Clara refrained from pulling the last from her handbag.

"I don't like that Clara," O'Harris' tone softened. "Some scoundrel sending you dirty notes and you'll be home alone tonight!"

"Not alone, I have Annie," Clara shrugged. "Besides, I am not intimidated."

O'Harris leaned on the back of his chair, scraping his fingers through his hair.

"I don't like it Clara," he repeated. "You could stay here?"

"It would not be proper, besides if I suspected my home might be attacked, I would not leave Annie there alone."

"Don't waste your breath old boy," Tommy interjected. "We've had this conversation already."

O'Harris looked at Clara with a strange misery in his eyes. It gave her goose-pimples on her arms.

"All right, I appreciate you won't stay. But you will let me escort you home, won't you?"

Clara was about to refuse, she resented people constantly thinking because she was a woman she was in permanent danger of attack, but the sadness in O'Harris' eyes softened her.

"Yes, you can escort me."

"Good, I'll show Tommy his room and then I'll make sure you get home safely."

Clara gave a faint nod; she didn't want to look at Tommy as he left the room, but her brother wasn't going to let her get away that easily. He thumped her hard on her upper arm, like when they were kids, and she automatically scowled at him.

"See you later, old girl. Have no fear," he winked at her, but no comfort he could offer would take the nagging feeling from her stomach that O'Harris and Tommy would get in that plane tomorrow and never return.

Half an hour later she was walking along the country lanes leading from O'Harris' house back to Brighton.

"You're really quite cross with me for asking Tommy to fly," O'Harris was plucking white blossoms off trees that lined the road.

"I can hardly be cross with you. It was Tommy's choice."

"But you are."

Clara made no reply.

"The *White Buzzard* is a creature of beauty Clara. I've never flown a plane like her. She feels her way through the air, she is a natural flier.

When I am in her I feel as though she is reacting to me before I even move a finger."

"Forgive me for being less enthusiastic."

"For four years I flew over the trenches in France and Belgium, Clara. Four long years and I never came a cropper. I was the pride of the Royal Flying Corps for it. Why should some piffling flight across the ocean be any different?"

"You don't see danger, O'Harris," Clara shook her head. "That scares me."

"You are not so good at seeing danger yourself. What of those letters?"

"Meaningless and I will find the writer soon enough."

"See what I mean? Other people would be worried you... you take it as a normal part of life. Perhaps that is where we are not so different. I am not afraid of flying."

"What about dying?"

"I'm not ready to pop my clogs yet. The *White Buzzard* will see me to America and back, don't you worry, and Tommy will be as safe as houses. I would not risk the wrath of his sister for anything."

He presented her with the small bundle of blossoms.

"Poor haul, but they are pretty," he said.

Clara took them and, despite herself, smiled.

"One day I will get you to fly with me Clara."

She laughed.

"Oh yes, and pigs might fly too! O'Harris the sky is not meant for the likes of me!"

"Why? Do you think you might find fault with it while you were up there?"

"I think it might find fault with me and cast me back down to earth!"

"Those are the words of a person who has never flown. When I come back, in a week's time, I shall take you for a flight."

"No, you won't!"

"Yes, I will, because I will make a promise now to you if you will make a promise too. If you promise with all your heart to let me take you for a flight when I return then I promise you that no power on this earth will prevent me from returning," he was smiling, but there was a spark in his eyes too.

Clara found her breath catching. It was only a promise but if she made it, just maybe, fate, God, luck, or chance, would hear her and ensure the safe return of O'Harris and her brother. A trip in a plane was such a minor thing to agree to in comparison to their safe return.

"All right, I shall promise."

"With all your heart?"

"Yes, with all my heart."

"Then I promise to return, that no power in this life will prevent me. I promise that with all my heart," O'Harris slapped his palm to his chest and grinned broadly.

And she believed him. She really did.

Chapter Twenty-Six

Saturday was cold with a faint drizzle in the air. Clara stood on the pier alone and gazed at the white aeroplane down on the sand. A handful of people milled about it, but the pilots were not with them, not yet. She glanced at her watch and realised there were many minutes to go before the plane soared into the skies. She couldn't bear the wait; she had been up half the night thinking of this moment. She walked the length of the pier and then back, more people gathering at the railings all the time. Finally, she moved to the empty far side and stared out into the sea.

"You here to see the magic happen too?"

She glanced up at Oliver Bankes and smiled.

"Hello Oliver."

"Hello Clara."

"You haven't gassed yourself then."

"Not yet," Bankes grinned broadly. "But I am inching closer to the perfect mix. I developed a plate of a row of houses and the shadows were so close to perfect it made me want to cry. Oh..."

Oliver blushed at what he had just said.

"I understand," Clara assured him. "We all have our passions and men do seem to become very absorbed in theirs."

"Ah, you refer to O'Harris," Oliver nodded to the other side of the pier. "Are you not watching?"

"I'm not sure I can."

"I have the camera set up, well actually I have two," Oliver pointed out two cameras set side by side. "The plan is I take a shot with camera one just before the plane is in my sights and then take a shot with camera two. I'm hoping that way I might get a decent photograph. I read about the idea in a photography journal."

"It is certainly inventive," Clara agreed, she turned around and perched on the railing instead of leaning on it.

"These images could be worth a fortune if he breaks the record, you know," Oliver was suddenly all serious. "I don't mean to sound coarse, but these days any extra money I can earn is a bonus. People don't seem to be thinking about portraits so much at the moment."

Oliver looked forlorn.

"Have you ever thought of expanding your line of work?" Clara asked.

"How? I already freelance for the police."

"What about the *Brighton Gazette*?"

Oliver mused on the matter.

"They rarely use photographs."

"I know," Admitted Clara. "But is that because they don't want to or because they don't have any to print? Go to the editor and convince him his sales would increase if he started printing photos of events around the town."

"People do like looking at themselves."

"They would buy the paper just for the chance of spotting themselves."

"And I could suggest he offer prints of the photos for interested parties. I could take a percentage for producing them."

"Sounds like a fine idea."

Oliver beamed at her again.

"You are a grand gal, Clara. Will you let me buy you a cup of tea after they take-off?"

"Maybe," Clara was half-hearted. "Tommy's in that plane."

"He'll be all right."

Clara suddenly looked so grim Oliver wished he could catch her in his arms and comfort her.

"This feels like when he went off to war," Clara's voice trembled slightly. "Only mother and father were alive then."

"I'm sure he will be fine," Oliver took her hand gently.

Clara almost cried; his kindness almost tipped her emotions over the brink.

"You better go take your photographs," she said, pushing him away before the tears fell.

Oliver looked forlorn and reluctantly left to tend to his cameras. Clara sat alone on the railing, surreptitiously dabbing at her eyes, and listening for the first roar of the plane's engines. People were talking excitedly, there were murmurings in the crowd and Clara picked up from odd phrases she overheard that the pilots had appeared. She held her breath. Down on the beach an engine thrummed into life, sand flew up into the crowd and Oliver cursed as it dusted his camera lens. The next instant the plane was moving, the noise changed almost imperceptibly, but the crowd began to cheer, and Clara knew they were starting their take off.

Moments passed; sand blew over again. The engine became a constant sound and then there was a strange whoosh and the noise fell a decibel. Clara glanced up instinctively at the same moment as Oliver took shots with his camera. A brilliant white plane soared up into the air, the sun dazzling off its skin. In the pilot seat, just visible, a man waved. Quietly Clara waved back and then it was flying out of sight, a stark white bird against the grey sky. It vanished within moments. Clara started to shake.

She felt Oliver's hand on hers.

"Shall I walk you home?"

She glanced up at his concerned face and made an effort to control herself. There would be no tears out here in public, she would mask all the terror she felt inside. But somehow, she couldn't quite let go of his hand.

"Yes," she said softly. "Walk me home."

Clara expected to enter a silent house, but when she opened the door with Oliver behind her, she heard voices and even a peal of female laughter coming from the kitchen. It seemed Annie had company and Clara felt a hot pang of anger that she could be so merry when the man she supposedly loved had just flown off. She marched down the hallway, forgetting Oliver who stood in the doorway wondering if he was invited in or not.

She stormed into the kitchen and came to a halt.

"My word old girl, you have a face like a thundercloud!"

Tommy grinned at her from the far side of the kitchen table.

"Thomas Eugene Fitzgerald!" Clara growled.

"Oh dear, I'm for it now chaps," Tommy glanced at Colonel Brandt who was with him at the table and was trying to appear as small as possible.

"Explain yourself!" Clara demanded.

To her right she noticed Annie who was trying to look serious, while masking her total elation that Tommy was safely sitting in the kitchen and not in a plane above Brighton.

"Calm down, dear sister. This is hardly the reaction I was expecting, aren't you pleased to see me?"

"I sat on that pier..." Clara was so furious it hurt to talk. "I thought... I nearly cried in public!"

"That is bad," Tommy nodded grimly. "I understand why you are so cross. Clara Fitzgerald does not show her emotions in public."

Then he couldn't help but laugh.

"Isn't this terribly horrid of me? Do you want the whole truth?"

"Yes, I do," Clara felt her temper receding.

"Ahem, before that, might we ask the nice young man standing at the front door to join us?" Interrupted Annie.

Clara glanced out the kitchen door and saw the distant figure of Oliver still loitering in the doorway. She felt a pang of annoyance that he couldn't be dynamic enough to take the initiative and come in. Captain O'Harris wouldn't have worried. She felt guilty as soon as the thought crossed her mind, it was because O'Harris didn't worry that he was quite happy to risk all and leave his friends behind to fly a plane.

"Oliver, do come in. It appears I have been the subject of a rather unpleasant joke," she called.

"Don't be mean Clara," Tommy laughed. "It wasn't so unpleasant."

Oliver joined them in the kitchen, lumping his cameras all the way.

"I say, what have you been up to?" Brandt glimpsed the cameras with enthusiasm.

"Taking shots of Captain O'Harris in the *White Buzzard*. Hang on, if Tommy is here who was the other man in the plane?"

"Exactly what I would like to know," Clara agreed. "Wait, no first I want to know exactly why you are sat at this table Thomas."

Tommy shrugged his shoulders.

"I had a change of heart," he suddenly looked abashed. "I suppose, what you said stuck with me. How what I might be leaving behind was worth more than the thrill of adventure."

His eyes wandered to Annie.

"Perhaps I lost my nerve too."

"Never that Tommy," Annie said softly.

"Well, I changed my mind and that is all that matters."

"When did you change your mind?" Clara demanded.

Tommy gave Brandt a worried glance.

"It wasn't as though it was a firm decision or anything..."

"When?"

"Day after that discussion with you," Tommy could no longer look directly into Clara's blazing eyes,

"I told O'Harris I wasn't up to it. Said I didn't have confidence in my health or some-such. He didn't entirely believe me, I dare say, but he accepted and said he had a man who might be able to take my place. Next, I heard it was all arranged, some chap named Digby was going with him."

"And you chose not to tell me?" Clara said.

"Welllll..." Tommy looked around for help, but everything was avoiding his gaze, "You see, I felt a bit, well, a bit peeved with everyone. I don't know. I felt as though after all the fuss I had made, if I then went and said I had changed my mind it would be a bit like you had won."

He stared at his sister.

"It would hardly have been like that," Clara responded, her anger was abating now even if she remained annoyed.

"It still would have felt like it. I persuaded O'Harris to keep my secret, he swore he would not mention a word that I had dropped out."

"And nor did he. Even yesterday he was acting as though you were flying with him," Clara went slightly cold at how easily O'Harris had lied to her, and she had not even realised. That was an unpleasant realisation for a detective.

"Colonel Brandt was in on it. He brought me home today, and I told Annie yesterday. She acted very much like you did at first."

"Now I just feel relieved," Annie hastily added.

"And that's it really. Here I am safe and sound," Tommy smiled at his sister. "Surely that is good?"

"You could have told me," Clara said, thinking of the sleepless nights she had endured.

"Why don't we all sit down and have a late breakfast," Annie, forever the peacemaker, intervened. "What matters most is that Tommy isn't up in that frightful plane."

"Did it take off all right?" Brandt asked now the conversation seemed to have turned a corner.

"Swooped up just like a bird," Oliver assured him. "I can't wait to develop these plates and see what shots I got. If they are good, I am going to sell them to the papers."

The others started to chatter companionably, but Clara found herself tongue-tied. She sat at the end of the table and caught Tommy's eye. He gave her a strange smile. She knew he understood. But for now, there was a breakfast of kippers and eggs and a warm pot of tea, and Brandt was confessing a fascination with photography to Oliver and being invited to come over to the studio while he developed the plates. All seemed harmonious again. Except for the flutter inside Clara's stomach.

Chapter Twenty-Seven

A week went by. It was quiet. Clara went to her office but there were no clients waiting for her. Instead, she found on her desk an envelope addressed to her in a hand she faintly recognised. She opened it and a cheque fell out. She looked at the amount and shook her head in alarm.

"Far too much you silly man," she now recognised the hand as that of O'Harris.

There was a letter accompanying the cheque. She unfolded it.

Dearest Clara,

You will swear when you see the cheque, yes, I know you shall, but it is all yours for a job well done, even if the answers stung a little. I can never express my gratitude for solving this mystery, you may not believe that, but I mean it. The truth, though horrid at first, is better than lie after lie. I am sorry for what my father did, I will never understand how he could arrange such an evil thing. All I can say is they were not the actions of the man I remember. Maybe you were right, maybe it was the cancer.

By the time you read this you are sure to know Tommy has not come with me, please forgive me for lying to you, I did not do it out of wickedness, but to be loyal to a friend. Yes, I consider Tommy a friend and you too Clara. I am extraordinarily pleased I met you two. Tommy has made me laugh and smile and reminded me what it is to be alive in the world again and you Clara, you have given me something to be alive for. A ray of hope, call it, if you will. When I soar in Buzzard *tomorrow, I expect to see you waving and I shall think of you throughout my flight. When I land, I shall declare I did this challenge because of the wonderful woman called Clara Fitzgerald and you will be furious to have your name brandished in the* New York Times, *I am sure!*

Please forgive me for that too!

One last thing before I leave off and try to gain a few hours' sleep before I take flight tomorrow. All this talk of Florence over the last few weeks made me think and I searched this house from top to bottom to find anything I might have missed. I thought it might help you. Well, I found this letter; it had slipped down the back of Florence's bedside table. I'm afraid I was cowardly Clara and could not give it to you at first, but I somehow doubt the information has passed you by. I enclose the letter with this one, for you to read at your leisure. When I return, please say no more about it. Some things are best left unspoken.

Take care Clara, I'll see you in a week or two.
Fond Regards
Captain John O'Harris

Clara found the letter unsettling. She couldn't explain why. It spoke so cheerfully and happily, almost a promise to return, yet that dread had engulfed her again. She put it to one side and shook off the thoughts.

Her attention fell on the second letter that had accompanied O'Harris.' The envelope was addressed to Florence and before she read the contents, she quickly looked for the author. Oscar O'Harris' signature, painfully drawn by a hand trembling from the disease about to snatch him away, appeared at the bottom. Clara's mouth went dry as she began to read.

Dear Florence,

This is a bitter-sweet missive. You have no time for me, of that I am acutely aware, and I assure you, dear lady, I feel a similar regard for you. So, it pains me little to write what I must and inform you of your husband's actions.

I have instructed my solicitor to give you this upon my death. Consider it a parting gift. For appearances' sake I have also left you a little something, we must not have the family's reputation tainted, after all. I wonder if you will stand at my funeral Florence? No doubt you shall, for to do otherwise would be to cast shame on the O'Harris name.

Not that my beloved brother Goddard has not already done that. I hope you show him this and I hope he has the gall to deny my words, no matter if he does, the truth is plain enough. I have been a fool, a stupid cuckold.

My only son and heir, a boy I have deeply loved and adored as a gift from God, is a contemptible joke. That I believed, (yes believed!) that I might actually have sired an heir despite what the doctors had told me sickens me, but not as much as it shall sicken you. I want you to join me in my suffering Florence, I want you to know my spite as I have known yours – the silences, the unspoken comments, the looks! I have seen them! You cannot deny them!

So now it is my turn. Upon her deathbed, my darling and beloved wife, who I cherished beyond anything, perhaps beyond what I should have, confessed to me the most awful of sins. Our son, who I praised each day as a miracle, was never our son. He was the son of Susan O'Harris and Goddard O'Harris.

Does that news make your stomach turn as it did mine? Does it make you stop and think about the 'doting uncle' act he played all those years? He knew, of course, he knew! He treated John just like a son because he was his son!

Then, here is my revenge. I only hope there is an afterlife so I might watch you read this. I shall take little pleasure, however, for I have been as big a fool as you. We are even now, Florence, and I am weary of the battle that rages within me.

Don't blame John, that is all I beg of you. He has nothing after I am gone, and I rely on you and Goddard to watch over him. How ironic I insult you and then ask for help? But it is not for me, it is for Goddard's son.

Farewell dear sister-in-law. I have no more words for you.

Oscar O'Harris.

Clara's heart was thudding in her chest as she sat down, the letter drifting from her fingers.

"He knows," and what a way he had learned the news; in a spiteful and cruel letter written by the man he had called father all his life.

Poor O'Harris. She shut her eyes, trying the impossible, to imagine what it must feel like to discover your father is not the man you had thought he was all these years.

Silently she stood, retrieved her belongings, and headed for home. She couldn't let this strange mixture of misery and shock simmer inside while she was trapped at her office. She would head home and show the letter to Tommy and ask him if he had had any indication that O'Harris knew. She tried to ignore the uneasy feeling in her stomach as she hurried home.

"Tommy?" She went into the drawing room, then the front parlour, "Tommy?"

"Kitchen, Clara!"

She followed his voice.

"I found a letter on my desk from O'Harris, Tommy it is awful, but he knows…" She paused just inside the kitchen.

Tommy was at the table and Colonel Brandt was with them. Annie was making strong tea and gave Clara a fraught look as she entered. There was a newspaper on the table.

"First news from America," Tommy said. "About O'Harris."

Clara thought he looked disappointed.

"He didn't break the record."

"No Miss Fitzgerald, no he didn't," Brandt shook his head sadly.

There was a long pause.

"Clara, the *White Buzzard* took a dive into the Atlantic," Tommy explained gently. "When it didn't arrive in America as expected the coastal authorities sent out a search party. They found Vauxhall Digby, the co-pilot, half-drowned but alive floating in his life jacket."

"But O'Harris…" Clara didn't need the answer, she had known it would be like this all along.

"They haven't found him. They presume him drowned," Tommy unfolded the paper carefully. "Digby says they hit an unexpected patch of bad weather which blew them off course and then the engine started to smoke. O'Harris tried all he could but something had choked the engine and the *Buzzard* just dropped like a stone."

"Those are the hazards of flying," Clara took a seat stiffly, she felt too calm at the news, too resigned. It scared her.

"Clara, I'm so glad you persuaded me not to go," Tommy was chewing on his lip anxiously. "If I had been in that plane, I... I would have drowned. With my bad legs and all."

"You weren't on the plane," Annie appeared and comforted him stoically. "You weren't meant to be on it."

"Digby will be all right?" Clara felt like someone else was talking in her voice, she felt distant and hollow.

"He will be fine, doctors say he has a slight case of exposure from being out in the sea, but nothing that won't improve with rest."

"This is a very sad day," Brandt said to no one in particular.

"Digby had a wife and kids, so at least he made it," Tommy said. "Clara, I'm..."

"Don't say anything, please," Clara stood and left the room. She went to her bedroom and lay on the bed staring at the ceiling.

"I wasn't in love with him," she told the air in the room. "Not like that. But I liked his friendship."

She rolled over and peered at the picture frames on her bedside cabinet. Her mother and father on their wedding day looked at her, smiling, and Tommy stood proudly in his army uniform. Why did this hurt so much? He was no more than an acquaintance, that was all.

For a long time, she felt numb and unsure of herself. Then a strange coil of anxiety tweaked at her conscience. She had known, hadn't she? She had felt this fate coming, felt the dread twisting her nerves and telling her it was all wrong. It was nonsense, of course, just the natural fears of the unknown, but what if... What if she could have saved him?

She shut her eyes and tried to escape into darkness, but there O'Harris seemed stronger than ever, his voice ringing out loudly, *well detective, you didn't do a good job of deciphering this, huh?*

"Go away," she hissed to herself, but the ghost of O'Harris loitered glaring at her until she opened her eyes and realised she had been lying there so long the afternoon was turning to evening.

Clara forced herself to get up. She would not be crippled by guilt over O'Harris, not when it was his own foolish decision to get in a plane and fly. She could not have convinced him to cancel the flight anyway, she had no power over him.

Clara made her way downstairs and into the dining room where there was a faint aroma of roast beef. Annie was just arranging the food on the table before she called everyone. She glanced up at Clara.

"I thought I might have to fetch you. Feel better?"

"I don't know," Clara took her usual place at the table and noticed there was an extra setting.

"I asked Colonel Brandt to stay for dinner," Annie told her. "The poor man doesn't have a soul at home except a housekeeper and that club is no place when you are feeling sorry for yourself."

Annie gave a look as if a club were a filthy place that she would never deem to enter even if she were allowed.

"I have no objections," Clara assured her.

"Good, because I thought you would do the same had you been here," Annie finished with setting out the food as she liked and then fussed with the tablecloth awkwardly. "Did you care for him?"

Clara raised and lowered her shoulders, but it was not exactly a shrug.

"That Oliver Bankes is a nice fellow," Annie continued.

It actually brought a half-smile to Clara's face.

"I know Annie."

"I can't say as O'Harris weren't a nice fellow as well," Annie added magnanimously. "But I shall never forgive him for asking my Tommy to go in that plane."

My Tommy, Clara noted.

"He was merely a friend," Clara said calmly. "It's just, somehow I feel I could have saved him."

"And you come by that nonsense how?" Annie said almost sternly.

"I had these feelings of dread about the flight."

"So did I, but I ain't saying I'm clairvoyant. Besides, I had the same feelings when my mum went into hospital with pneumonia. I quite convinced myself she wasn't coming back, yet she did. And I didn't feel a thing before that bomb crashed down on our house, I could have used a feeling of dread then. Haven't you ever had experiences like that?"

Clara had.

"Now you mention it, I felt the same way when Tommy went on a boating holiday with his friends down the Norfolk broads. He was only sixteen or seventeen, I suppose. Some of the other lads were older. I was certain there would be an accident, but he came home all right."

"There you are. Don't go mixing normal feelings with anything superstitious. You could have done nothing about it. The captain was going to fly whether you agreed with it or not and to say anything else is to drive yourself insane."

"You have a wise head on you, Annie."

Annie snorted.

"It's because I have to put up with you two all day. Someone has to be rational in this house."

"Do I hear my name being scorned in vain?" Tommy wheeled himself into the room.

"I only tell it as it is," Annie said staunchly. "Now get yourselves seated and I'll serve up. Colonel Brandt do sit here, else you'll be in the draught from the door when I go in and out."

The colonel looked particularly glum as he entered the room but brightened slightly as Annie fussed about him.

"I've made a lovely thick gravy," Annie told him. "And there are Yorkshire puds and dumplings."

"You are a little marvel," the colonel managed a smile. "I'm glad to see you up again Clara."

"I felt a touch unwell."

"I understand."

Clara felt the colonel was trying to understand too much, he gave her a knowing smile and she felt uncomfortable.

"Clara, I was telling the Colonel about those notes of yours," Tommy interrupted as Annie served everyone with beef and potatoes. "We've been thinking about them."

"Yes, I must say I found them very disturbing," the colonel looked grave. "To think someone would write such things to a lady."

Clara was touched, especially as few people called her a lady since she took on being a private detective.

"We've been creating a 'profile' for the suspect," Tommy added.

"Beg your pardon?" Clara looked blank.

"It's an American thing, you create a description of the person who was behind the crime based on the clues you have. They call it a profile."

"I think it rather sounds like something Sherlock Holmes would have done," the colonel nodded, a little colour returning to his cheeks.

"And this 'profile' leads you to the suspect?"

"It narrows things down," Tommy told her. "You don't mind I rooted in your handbag for that last note you got, do you? I saw you put it in there and it was a piece of evidence, and I didn't want to disturb you."

Tommy actually looked abashed, no doubt he had searched without even thinking about what he was doing until afterwards. Clara was in no mood to argue.

"I suppose I cannot mind what has been done, and as it was to my benefit, I see no reason to complain. Did it help at all?"

"Well, actually, it did," Tommy nodded to the colonel. "Perhaps you should explain, Colonel."

The colonel noticeably hesitated, then a new spark lit his eyes.

"I dare say you have already figured this all-out Miss Fitzgerald. I am bound to be way behind the times."

Clara smiled at him gently.

"Try me," she said.

"Well, I looked at the papers you had received, and my first thoughts were how scruffy they were. You noticed the fingerprints?"

"Yes, very black, but smudged."

"But we agree the person who wrote the notes had dirty hands and had not bothered to wash them before writing the messages?"

"Yes, I agree with that."

"I think that would imply a person who routinely has dirty hands and, as such, fails to notice them in the manner that a person with routinely clean hands, who just happened to have got their hands dirty, would."

"I can't fault the logic to that," Clara nodded. "So, you suggest a person in an industry where their hands would be regularly dirty?"

"Yes, now that may help you already, but I looked at the notes further. I have to say the person's handwriting did not impress me, but at the same time I realised it was by a person who had had some level of education. The writing may have been untidy but there were no errors."

"A literate person," Clara agreed again.

"Then I looked at the paper itself and it struck me that that was most significant. As Tommy pointed out most people when writing a note will use materials they have to hand, not go out and buy something especially. This paper was rather thick and had a waxed, greasy surface. It didn't strike me as good writing paper and the way the author had dug hard into it with his pencil seemed to suggest he was also aware of its downfalls."

"Any idea where such a paper would be used?" Clara asked.

"That's where I come back in," Tommy returned to the narrative. "Both the Colonel and I mused over the paper for some time and then it occurred to me I had seen just such a paper before. While I was recuperating at that old hospital the nurses liked to find us little tasks to keep ourselves occupied and one of these tasks was growing flowers from seeds. The seeds came in a brown paper packet with a name on it and inside the packet the more delicate seeds were folded in a slip of waxed paper. You could use the paper to write labels for the plants on and it would last in the rain long enough for the plants to shoot and be identifiable."

Clara looked hard at her brother, then she caught her breath.

"Mr Riggs," she sat back in her chair. "I suspected him, but I could not connect him with the messages. And then there is the why? And how did he get past the cook and put the dead mouse in the pâté?"

"But it has to be him, doesn't it?"

"I must run this past the inspector," Clara collected her thoughts. "This is serious and must be dealt with by the police."

"Clara, what are you thinking?"

"Florence O'Harris did not move her husband's body. Colonel Brandt did not move the body. Only one other person has confessed to being on the scene at the time and that same person has been sending me notes to leave things alone. Mr Riggs was involved somehow, not in the actual murder, unless he had some correspondence with Oscar O'Harris, but certainly it seems with concealing the body."

Clara put down her knife and fork.

"Yes, this is serious. I may be able to actually find the body of poor Goddard O'Harris."

Chapter Twenty-Eight

Mr Riggs was giving a preventive douse of fungicide to his roses in case of black spot when he caught sight of Clara Fitzgerald. She was entering the garden from the side door accompanied by a tall, official looking man. He ignored them. Rumours of the captain's demise had yet to reach him, and he assumed they were there on matters relating to O'Harris. Even so, he couldn't help a pang of anxiety as they walked right up to him.

"Good morning, Mr Riggs, your roses look well," Clara said jauntily. "This is Inspector Park-Coombs."

The inspector tipped his hat.

"We've come to have a word Mr Riggs," Clara spoke as she bent down to pick something off the ground, it was a slip of paper Mr Riggs had been making jottings on. "A formula?"

"It's the recipe for my black spot spray," Mr Riggs answered. "My own blend."

He watched uncomfortably as Clara handed the paper to the inspector and the policeman withdrew a handful of other papers from his pocket. He compared them at length.

"You wrote this note?" The inspector enquired, holding up the paper with the fungicide recipe.

"I did," Riggs admitted. "Is this about the chemicals I use? They are all legal and bought from the chemist."

"No, it's not about that Mr Riggs," the inspector looked grim. "You know very well what it is about."

He held the three threatening notes before the gardener.

"Do you recognise these?"

"Can't say I do."

"They are in your handwriting, Mr Riggs, I just compared it to your recipe which you declare was written by you."

"That may be…"

"They also have fingerprints on them, and should I compare them to your fingerprints, which I could do very easily back at my station, I believe I would find a match."

Mr Riggs looked sick to his stomach. He glanced at Clara and was surprised to see she looked sad.

"Why did you send them Mr Riggs?" She asked, "You swore you had no connection with Millie the maid, or the murder of Goddard. So why?"

"Millie?" Mr Riggs was astounded. "Murder? I had no doings with that maid, and I never laid a finger on my master. I was fond of him. He was good to me."

"But you had something to do with it, didn't you?" Clara insisted. "You moved his body."

"I never…"

"Someone moved Goddard O'Harris that evening, only three people were present and two of them are accounted for. That leaves you Mr Riggs and, if you had nothing to do with the crime, whatsoever, why send me notes trying to persuade me to stop?"

Mr Riggs' face was contorted into a grimace of misery. He looked at the notes the inspector still held before him and knew he was done for.

"Will they hang me?" He asked, trembling.

"Not for sending notes," the inspector assured him. "But I do need the full story, or it will go very hard for you."

"It isn't like you think," Mr Riggs fumbled with his gardening gloves. "I never harmed anyone."

"So why?" Clara demanded.

"Because you wanted to find the body so badly," Mr Riggs shook his head. "And if you had of done, that would have been just awful."

"You did move the body then?"

"Yes," Mr Riggs gasped out loud. "I come upon Goddard right here."

He pointed at the path between his rose bushes.

"He was dead, I knew that as soon as I saw him and just like I told you there was Florence O'Harris in the doorway and she was telling me she had called for a doctor. Then she vanished inside. I told you I walked away, but that isn't true. Because as I looked down at Goddard, I realised he had fallen with his arms in my roses. I only wanted to move him so I could see if there were any damage, but when I did, it was just awful."

Mr Riggs looked horror-struck; Clara felt a chill run down her spine. Had she missed something?

"What was awful Mr Riggs?" Pursued the inspector.

"Where he had fallen, my roses, they were withered and dead! A whole three bushes, fine ones too, big ones. One was a late bloomer, and the roses were curled up and shrivelled on the branch, it was horrible," Mr Riggs closed his eyes at the shock of the memory.

"Arsine gas," Clara mouthed to the inspector. Park-Coombs nodded.

"Then what, Mr Riggs?"

"Well, Mr O'Harris was in the way, I couldn't get to my roses to see if anything could be done, this path is rather narrow. So, I just pulled him out of the way, but when I stopped, I realised what I had done, and he looked so... dead. I couldn't have him there staring at me while I fixed the roses, he gave me the jitters. I dragged him further away and rolled him into the ha-ha. I meant to tell Mrs O'Harris as soon as I got back from my shed with some nitrogen treatments for the roses. But I was away a while mixing some up and when I came back there were the police and I heard them talking about murder and the vanished body and a crime being committed, and I thought I would be in a lot of trouble. No one had noticed me, so I hurried back to my shed."

"The body didn't stay in the ha-ha though?"

"No. As soon as everyone had gone, and the house had quietened down I wondered what to do. It seemed to me confessing I had moved him would look very bad, especially with Colonel Brandt calling out things like murder. I sat for a bit and thought, and it occurred to me if they couldn't find the body then the matter would be over and no one need know I was there," Mr Riggs gave a deep sigh. "I had to dig those dead roses up anyway, and all the occupied bedrooms are on the front of the house, so no one would notice me. I took up the dead roses, pitiful things they were and threw them into my barrow and then I dug a deep trench, and I pulled Mr O'Harris from the ha-ha. He was all stiff and awful, but I did it and I tipped him into the trench with my apologies, I ain't an unchristian man, you know, and I said a prayer over him.

"Then I started to fill the trench and I realised the missing roses could look odd and people might nose in the soil. I didn't have any spare roses, so I did something that nearly broke my heart all over again. I dug up live roses from both sides of the path and I spaced them all about and replanted them, so the trench would be covered and there would be no obvious gaps. Once it was all done it was nearly dawn and I went back to my cottage and fell asleep."

In unison Clara and the inspector looked downwards.

"Goddard O'Harris is buried here?" Clara pointed to a pretty tea rose.

"Yes, and I just knew if you found out you would insist on digging him up and my roses would be ruined again. You don't know how hard it is to transplant a well-grown rose. I almost lost the lot the last time and police detectives are messy diggers," Mr Riggs was almost in tears. "I never hurt Mr O'Harris, and I never wished him harm, I just wanted my roses to be safe."

"I'm sorry Mr Riggs, but he will have to be dug up."

"No!" Mr Riggs gave a sob.

"You're lucky I'm not arresting you for being an accessory to a murder!" Cautioned the inspector. "As it is Clara has persuaded me it is not worth my time arresting you and she isn't pressing charges over the notes. I've got some bobbies round the front; I'll have them digging in a jiffy."

Mr Riggs looked miserably at Clara.

"I am sorry," he said.

"I know. Just one thing, the mouse?"

"I snuck it in while cook was busy in the herb garden. I took off my boots so as she wouldn't notice the dirt."

Clara nodded.

"I suspected as much. Might I suggest Mr Riggs you go find some very big containers that we can fill with water? I shall do my best to marshal the police into digging carefully and if we put the rose bushes into temporary pots, we might be able to save them, don't you think?"

Mr Riggs brightened slightly.

"That we might," he turned to obey her instructions, then paused. "You're more understanding than I expected. I should have known when I talked to you. I recognised a fellow gardener, but this is kindness beyond what I could have hoped for."

"Fetch those containers Mr Riggs," Clara smiled. The gardener hurried off.

The digging took an hour, with Clara insisting the policemen took care around the roots of the rose bushes and earning several grumbles and groans in the process. As each rose was uprooted it was placed in various containers Mr Riggs had found; one was placed in an old wash tub, another in a rusty tin bath. Slowly the ground was excavated, and the men dug deeper.

It was midday and the inspector was enjoying an egg and ham sandwich from a platter cook had prepared for the workers when a policeman gave a cry for him to come over. Clara had been sitting on the steps to the dining room, idle in her thoughts, but ran over when she heard the cry. Someone had rustled up a brush and was sweeping away the last crumbs of soil from a white skull. Clara stared at the remains of Goddard O'Harris. She had found him.

"It's a shame the captain can't be around to see this," the inspector said softly.

Clara felt her chest tighten as she thought of Captain O'Harris' own body lost somewhere at sea. That, she would never find.

"You've solved the mystery," the inspector said, noticing her glumness. "Aren't you pleased?"

"Goddard can finally be laid to rest with Florence, and we know how he died at last, yes that is good, and I am pleased."

"But?"

Clara paused.

"I suppose I always imagined Captain O'Harris to be here for this moment. That he is not, is… wrong."

"I'm sorry about that."

Clara didn't want to dwell on the matter.

"It is all over, at last. Florence O'Harris can rest without her name being tarnished by gossips and though no one will see justice for this we at least now know what happened to Goddard O'Harris."

"Well, I suppose I shall be organising a funeral."

"Remember to invite me and Colonel Brandt."

"That I shall, is the Colonel doing all right?" They strolled together across the garden, away from the skeleton.

"He is doing fine. I believe he has become another of Annie's waifs and strays, and she shall do all in her power to ensure he is looked after."

"Another?"

"Surely Inspector, by now you realise I and my brother were Annie's first charity cases."

The inspector laughed stoutly.

"I have never known someone with such a peculiar household arrangement!"

"Hardly that," Clara pretended to look offended.

"Well, you surprise me at every turn Clara Fitzgerald. I do look forward to your next case."

"Whenever that may be," Clara shrugged. "Perhaps I shall take the summer off."

"Nonsense Clara, you are like a policeman. Trouble finds you, not the other way around."

They both turned and stared back at the big house.

"I suppose it will be sold."

"That is probably just as well," Clara gazed up at the big windows of the house. "Captain O'Harris told me the place held ghosts for him."

She watched as a flicker of sunlight played on a pane of glass and for a moment seemed to make a face appear at the window.

"I think he was more right than he realised."

Enjoyed this Book?

You can make a difference

As an independent writer reviews of my books are hugely important to help my work reach a wider audience. If you haven't already, I would love it if you could take five minutes to review this book on Amazon.

Thank you very much!

The Clara Fitzgerald Series

Have you read them all?

Memories of the Dead
The first mystery

Flight of Fancy
The second mystery

Murder in Mink
The third mystery

Carnival of Criminals
The fourth mystery

Mistletoe and Murder
The fifth mystery

The Poison Pen
The sixth mystery

Grave Suspicions of Murder
The seventh mystery

The Woman Died Thrice
The eighth mystery

Murder and Mascara
The ninth mystery
The Green Jade Dragon
The tenth mystery
The Monster at the Window
The eleventh mystery
Murder on the Mary Jane
The twelfth mystery
The Missing Wife
The thirteenth mystery
The Traitor's Bones
The fourteenth mystery
The Fossil Murder
The fifteenth mystery
Mr Lynch's Prophecy
The sixteenth mystery
Death at the Pantomime
The seventeenth mystery
The Cowboy's Crime
The eighteenth mystery
The Trouble with Tortoises
The nineteenth mystery
The Valentine Murder
The twentieth mystery
A Body Out of Time
The twenty-first mystery
The Dog Show Affair
The twenty-second mystery
The Unlucky Wedding Guest
The twenty-third mystery

Worse Things Happen at Sea
The twenty-fourth mystery
A Diet of Death
The twenty-fifth mystery
Brilliant Chang Returns
The twenty-sixth mystery
Storm in a Teacup
The twenty-seventh mystery
The Dog Theft Mystery
The twenty-eighth mystery
The Day the Zeppelin Came
The twenty-ninth mystery
The Mystery of Mallory
The thirtieth mystery

Also by Evelyn James

The Gentleman Detective Series

The Gentleman Detective

Norwich 1898.

Colonel Bainbridge, private detective, is wondering if it is time to hang up his magnifying glass when the arrival of his niece and the unexpected death of a pugilist has him trying to prove a man innocent of murder.

Delving into the murky world of street fighting and match fixing, can they determined who really killed the boxer Simon One-Foot or will a man who has done no wrong end up swinging for a crime he could not have committed?

Available on Amazon

About the Author

Evelyn James (aka Sophie Jackson) began her writing career in 2003 working in traditional publishing before embracing the world of ebooks and self-publishing. She has written over 80 books, available on a variety of platforms, both fiction and non-fiction.

You can find out more about Sophie's various titles at her website **www.sophie-jackson.com** or connect through social media on Facebook **www.facebook.com/SophieJacksonAuthor** and if you fancy sending an email do so at **sophiejackson.author@gmail.com**

Copyright © 2023 by Evelyn James

First published by Red Raven Publications 2014

This edition 2023

All rights reserved.

The moral right of Evelyn James to be identified as the author of this work has been asserted by her in accordance with the Copyright, Designs and Patents Act 1988.

All the characters in this book are fictitious, and any resemblance to actual persons living or dead is purely coincidental.

No part of this publication may be reproduced, stored in a retrieval system or transmitted in any form or by any means, without the prior permission in writing of the publisher, nor to be otherwise circulated in any form of binding or cover other than that in which it is published without a similar condition, including this condition, being imposed on the subsequent purchaser.

Evelyn James is a pen name for Sophie Jackson.

To contact about licensing or permission rights email sophiejackson.author@gmail.com

Printed in Great Britain
by Amazon